Notes

Also By K. B. Dixon:

Novel Ideas
The Photo Album
The Ingram Interview
A Painter's Life
Andrew (A to Z)
The Sum of His Syndromes
My Desk and I

A NOVEL

~

K. B. Dixon

Cover and interior design by Jayme Vincent | Inkwater.com

Abstract Musical Background © Ghen. BigStockPhoto.com

This is a work of fiction. The events described here are imaginary. The settings and characters are fictitious or used in a fictitious manner and do not represent specific places or living or dead people. Any resemblance is entirely coincidental.

Publisher: Baffling Bay Books

ISBN 978-1-7346759-6-2

1 3 5 7 9 10 8 6 4 2

For Sandra Jean

July

JULY 22

Just received a note that the camera I ordered has been shipped. Very excited. Have been waiting almost two months now. It is a new sort of camera—a small one that is good for street shooting and low-light work, a camera that the mentor class of industry flacks has insisted will change my life. Am hoping it's the tool I need, the one that will help me make the sort of pictures I've been wanting to make—pictures that are related stylistically to the sort I have been making, but better.

Heard Stephen Booker is ill and has been let go from his teaching position. I haven't seen much of him lately. Emily thinks he is a bad influence—a pessimist who encourages in me a native inclination to despair.

Man shoots Seattle bus driver in rush hour.
Missing Iowa border collie found stuck in tree.

JULY 23

There is a new editor at *The Left Coast*. His name is Alan Boyle. He has been brought in to save the magazine—make it popular, profitable, efficient. He's an ambitious man. He won't be around long. He will move on, I'm sure, to something grander—something with a larger circulation; something that uses better, shinier paper; something that puts pictures of A-list Hollywooders on the cover. He has been regally indifferent to me and my work, sees music reviews (at least reviews of classical music) as filler—the sort of thing you use to keep one high-concept story from bumping into another. Wouldn't mind seeing him fail, but the magazine is not on firm ground. If he goes, it might go with him so I have to wish him well. I have the distinct feeling he would prefer me to be a little more deferential.

∾

Note to Self: Clean off table in garage.

∾

Hundreds evacuated amid Idaho wildfires.
Billboards give wrong date for Detroit election.

JULY 24

Downtown for lunch. Pair of lackluster tacos. Ran into a bearded man over on Alder who looked very much like Jesus. He had a large green parrot perched on his shoulder—a parrot he talked to constantly and kissed on the beak from time to time. He wanted me to know the bird's name was Oscar.

∾

Preface

This short diary (my first and last) was an experiment, an attempt to create a sort of baseline document that could be used to compare one's lived life (recorded however haphazardly in real-time) to one's remembered life—an instructive document that would corroborate or contradict certain impressions I have at the moment of the me I presently know, impressions I rely on to make daily decisions both large and small. To that end, I am afraid, it has proven only marginally helpful.

David Bacon

Think I'm making a new friend: Christine Mitchell. We have been talking a lot lately. We met at a library lecture on Herman Melville. She's part of the local literary scene. Has been for a long time. She runs with a crowd I do not—the mainstream, moneymaking crowd: people who receive advances from their publishers, people who sell their film rights to companies in California. I know her meticulous work and respect it. She looks on me and my peculiar productions, I think, as harmless, down-market exotica.

∾

One man stabbed in fight on MAX train near zoo.
2 Italian climbers die in Mont Blanc avalanche.

JULY 25

Had physical today. Have not had one in four years. I would not be having this one, but Emily extorted it. Doctor was new to me—Michael Lesser. (The old one was new four years ago. Remember nothing about him except that he was short, bespectacled, and socially inept.) He—Lesser—is tall, condescending, and monomaniacally dedicated to electronic record-keeping. You do not give him a medical history, you give him a data set. His diagnoses (whatever they may be) will not be the product of experience, knowledge, and intuition, but of algorithms. One senses in the painfully careful answers to even the most casual questions the spectral presence of a legal representative.

∾

Actor's custody case sparks parental-rights fight.
Clashes in Cairo as political crisis drags on.

JULY 26

Ran into Abbie, our next door neighbor, at the coffee shop. She has gotten thinner if that's possible. (She's two lost pounds away from appearing bulimic.) She is just back from a stay in Boston where she had her fourth knee operation. We talked about it briefly, as we always do, pretending to be friends. The subject consumes her as you would expect. She is young, single, and burdened with a seemingly irreparable injury. It amazes me that she never seems bitter.

Called Booker today to see how he was doing. We almost made a movie together once—a short thing about an institutionalized man who thought his wife was an insurance company spy. He wrote the script; I wrote the music. I was upset by the news of his illness, but I don't think I was as upset as I should have been. My powers of empathy are not what they used to be. Scheduled lunch.

∾

Driver in deadly I-5 crash now faces felony charge.
Black hole paradox may undercut Einstein theory.

JULY 27

Movie. Mediocre. Apparently this is the best a sentient adult can hope for in the summer. Lead actor did not think a menacing glare could be overused.

∾

Ham-and-cheese sandwiches in the park. Took picture (only decent one of the day) of fastidious woman with a silk orchid in her hair.

∾

Ran into Mrs. Hampton (Maureen) at the communal mailboxes. She is a small, birdlike woman who seems to be afraid of pretty much everything. She was telling me this evening about a mysterious footprint she found in her garden. She thinks someone might have been trying to break into her house.

∾

Note to Self: Refill soap dispensers in bathroom and kitchen.

∾

Woman gives birth to baby boy on flight to France.
Long-time president quits J.C. Penney board.

JULY 28

Remedial essay in the *Times* Book Review about how disappointing authors can be, how one should think twice about looking into various biographies. I agree. There is no better way to damage a prized illusion.

~

Grocery shopping. Asparagus, chicken, dried cranberries, ice cream.

~

Yard work at Emily's behest. An hour trimming the roses and jasmine. She enjoys this sort of thing, this being outside—the digging and snipping, the spraying and manicuring. For me it has become of late a tainted, disheartening, Sisyphean task.

~

Cannot shake my unhappiness with the last chamber piece. I've been trying to for months, but to no avail. It's like a ringing in the ears. I should never have written it. I should have moved on to something else.

~

Gunman takes 3 hostages at L.A. bank.
Talk-show diva flaunts her much slimmer figure.

JULY 29

New camera has arrived. It is currently hidden in a closet somewhere awaiting August 24 when it will reappear as my birthday present.

~

Working on three pieces at the moment (all in the early stages): fractured fugue, song cycle, and "The Coward" quartet. Which, if any, of these projects will be completed?

∾

Rabbits glow green for medical research.
Postal Service revamps Priority Mail program.

JULY 30

Haircut today. Another half-hour with Beth, the stylist, telling me tales of her sullen daughter, Phoebe, and her incontinent Chihuahua, Norman (a depressed and depressing little rescue dog who sleeps curled-up in a mouse-colored bed near the shampoo station). Another half-hour of struggling to make small talk—something I do not do very well at all.

∾

California lawmakers urge pension funds to halt Russian investments.
Fla. boy infected with "brain-eating" amoeba.

JULY 31

Received pair of silver gelatin prints ordered for portfolio—a Russian-looking chess player and a luxuriously bearded panhandler holding cardboard sign reading "Need $ for Beer."

Am pleased with them. A good picture is like a good melodic line—and for me, as rare.

∾

Lunch with Booker. He looked good, better than I expected, fleshier—but he's now wearing rancid cologne. It was a palpable presence at the table. I could taste it. Conversation was haphazard and wandering. Got the feeling that Stephen is now, for some reason, fundamentally confused.

∾

Note to Self: Embrace the unfamiliar.

∾

Four bottle bombs found near Sherwood school.
Thai officials seize illegal ivory at airport.

August

AUGUST 1

First rain in more than a month. Cooler temperatures and charcoal overcast made me hungry for fall.

∾

Talked with Sarah about the show in November. Wanted to be sure there would be no logistical problems at the scheduled close as I was going to be out of town. She said there should be no problems at alI. Have no excuse now for backing out.

∾

Dozens gather to honor slain graffiti artist.
American superstar wins Roger's Cup in romp.

AUGUST 2

Have been struggling for a while with Bailey's biography of Cheever and am on the edge of calling it quits. I have had pretty much all I can take of the drunken jackassery. I suspect I'm leaving C at rock bottom (pg. 480), but that's just going to have to be the way it is. I don't have the readerly stamina to go another 300+ pages, to stay with him through the miraculous recovery to the tragic end—through the drying out, the repenting, the dying too young.

∾

Perseid meteor shower should dazzle.
6 alarm fire destroys home in Turner.

AUGUST 3

Attended West Coast Beard and Mustache Championships. Was an even stranger world than I expected. Not a world of beards (and mustaches) and the people who grew, tended, and exhibited them, but a world of phantasmagorical beards (and mustaches) and the people who grew, tended, and exhibited them. No one objected to having their picture taken. In fact, just the opposite. The posing was shameless.

∾

US man detained in N. Korea hospitalized.
Libyan TV anchor shot dead.

AUGUST 4

Exercise, grocery shopping.

∾

Jeff Whately bought himself a racehorse—a racehorse named Balderdash. (Sold real-estate company and needed something to spend his money on.) Thinks it is the sport of kings. ASPCA would disagree.

∾

Christine came by the house. Was overly interested, I think, in the contents of my office. What detail registered and will represent to her my fatal flaw? How accurate will her interpretation be?

∾

Asian stocks gain as investors buy "cheap" China shares. Divorced couple's legal feud lasts 17 years.

AUGUST 5

Carted camera around all day for nothing. After a weekend with the beardos I doubt even an extra-terrestrial would have caught my eye.

∾

Our mysterious neighbors to the west have reappeared, confirming my hypothesis that they had not moved out surreptitiously in the middle of the night but were simply away on some sort of extended vacation.

∾

Note to self: Glue heel on Emily's shoe.

∾

Vice-President defends NSA surveillance programs.
Sherwood ranked 5th-best small town in US.

AUGUST 6

Gene and Barbara over for dinner. Pizza, ice cream, couple of bottles of wine. G looks good. Still recovering from surgery and treatment. Was away from his electronics business for a long time. Things are tight financially. Dinner conversation was, for the most part, focused on the arcana of health insurance—access, providers, coverage, etc., etc. They are remarkable people, the Rossis. Preternaturally resilient.

North Carolina ushers in restrictive voting laws.
Entrepreneur unveils plan for high-speed train.

AUGUST 7

Note from Holly. She wants to have lunch sometime in early September. I'm supposed to choose the day. My guess is she will want to eat at that deep-fried dive she likes off of Hwy 26.

Emily had an argument today with an autocrat at work who read my essay on Haydn and was insisting (belligerently) that the character of Maria, Haydn's wife, had been fictionalized and modeled on her. Emily tried to explain that this was not the case, that Maria had not been imaginatively decorated but based *in toto* on existing (if sketchy) reports. He, of course, knew better.

∾

Small plane lands on Delaware road.
Bigger hospitals may bring bigger bills for patients.

AUGUST 8

Emily had fingernails done today. Alice, the manicurist, entertained her with a long and squalid story of having her ancient home replumbed. Story featured a yard full of rusting pipes, a disappearing plumber, and a two-day job that was now three weeks old. (She has run a garden hose into the basement for a make-shift shower.)

∾

How long does a cantaloupe last in the refrigerator?

∾

Medtronic buys Cardiocom.
Colts linebacker Hickman likely out for the season.

AUGUST 9

Listened to television moderator and her panel of pundits talk about the possibility of another ignorant, mean-spirited Republican's presidential candidacy. He is a ridiculous person, but the controlling conceit is that he should not be treated as one because this show—like most of its sort—is simply desperate for subjects.

∾

Dogs help sniff out ovarian cancer in Pa. study.
Transgender teen murdered by mob in Jamaica.

AUGUST 10

Finished very rough draft of four-voiced fugue tentatively titled "Captions." Second section chaotically cluttered with surfeit of episodes.

∾

Jim and Mia over for dinner. Rotisseried chicken and cupcakes. Made them sit through slide show of our trip to France. Talked for a while about the music business. Jim's new recording is doing ok. He would, of course, like it to be doing ok-er. The end of the evening was dedicated to theorizing—the sort of thing three bottles of wine makes inevitable.

∾

Tony-winning theater legend dies.
Typhoon batters Philippines; 23 fishermen missing.

AUGUST 11

Usual Sunday morning: *Times*, exercise, grocery store.

∾

Afternoon walk around the lake. Am in a middling mood. Emily having trouble with her left leg.

∾

Father kills son and self during supervised visit.
Abducted teen spotted hiking in pjs.

AUGUST 12

Received birthday camera early. Took it downtown. Got a few shots I liked. One of a housepainter on his lunch break; another of a Marilyn Monroe look-alike. Focus seems a little slow. Image quality, though, is first-rate.

∾

Boston mobster guilty on 31 out of 32 counts.
Induced labor linked to autism.

AUGUST 13

Tossed a piece in the garbage this morning—an essay about writing sonatas or, more accurately, an essay about not writing sonatas. It was a catalogue of explanations—explanations of why I had abandoned one idea or another ("didn't feel lucky," "haunted by ghosts of similar idea that failed in the past," etc., etc). Product of chemical imbalance perhaps.

∾

Search continues for missing Polish national on Mt. Hood.
Dad cited for leaving baby in hot car.

AUGUST 14

There is a mood in *The Left Coast* offices today. Boyle, in a gratuitously malevolent exercise of power, has fired one of the copy editors, Olivia Schiff. The message sent was clear: the era of comfortable collegialism was over and a new one of fearful fiscalism has begun.

∾

Prints arrived from Massachusetts lab today. Look pretty good. Two portraits (man in bow tie, young lady wearing heart-shaped sunglasses). Should finish up preliminary portfolio.

∾

Went with Whately to the track to watch Balderdash train for a small local race. Ran into Billy Wills. Billy is a fake good-guy. Has an "aw-shucks" routine that is both consummate and craven.

∾

UPS cargo jet crash in Ala. kills 2.
Ohio prison to raise trout for zoo penguins.

AUGUST 15

First review of my new chamber piece appeared online today. It is the third piece of mine that this particularly generous reviewer has written about. Says my stuff always makes him feel smarter. He has a significant internet presence so I expect a small (very small) bump in sales. Anticipate this trickle of attention will continue for a few months—though, of course, “trickle” would qualify, I think, as a hyperbolic description of the likely response. Feel strangely divorced from the proceedings. Seems a waste of time, energy, and hope to seek an audience at this late date.

∾

Woman loses arm in Hawaii shark attack.
Oil reforms in Mexico may upend markets.

AUGUST 16

Found Voodoo Doughnut truck parked in square today. Picked up two boxes of assorted inspirations. Their shop over on Second St. always has a line running out the door and halfway down the block. I might wait that long for a kidney, but not for a bear claw. Anyway, we now have a pile to pass around. Expect to be sick this evening.

∾

Reading the Warrant book on photography in bits and pieces. It’s essentially a long-form advertisement for the man himself. Easy to imagine it as a polysyllabic parody of relentless self-regard.

∾

4 bodies found in sunken India submarine.
Thousands honor Elvis at Graceland vigil.

AUGUST 17

Received in the mail a report from my doctor on the lab tests that were run as part of my physical. "Urinalysis was without significant abnormality," "Complete blood count was without significant abnormality," "Cholesterol levels optimal," "Triglycerides, 47," etc., etc. I am supposed to be interested in all of this, but I am not. The letter is for Emily, to ease her mind. Her constant concern for my health is understandable (given her medical history), but it can be oppressive.

∾

Thieves steal Aumsville man's tools worth 20k.
Utility trying to contain spill in Mary's River.

AUGUST 18

Times, breakfast, exercise, grocery store, walk around Mill Pond, British mystery movie, work on miserable quartet, wine.

∾

Note to self: Send thank-you card to Caroline.

∾

Angry elephant attacks safari vehicle.
Petition to recall San Diego mayor begins.

AUGUST 19

They are doing repair work on the house across the street—which means, of course, a lot of hammering and hollering. Just the sort of thing one needs. Music for masochists.

∾

Does our new shampoo smell better than our old shampoo?

∾

Eruptions coat Japanese city with ash.
Lyme disease rates 10 times higher than previously reported.

AUGUST 20

Packing for Seattle trip.

∾

Met Mrs. Hampton at the mailboxes again. She talked to me for fifteen minutes about the stairs in her house. Apparently they are steep, and she is afraid of falling down them.

∾

Woke up to plangent howl. E flat, I think.

∾

Woman "dead" 42 minutes brought back to life.
Telescope captures dramatic moment of starbirth.

AUGUST 21

Train to Seattle. Favorite way to travel.

∾

First things first. Restaurants. Wine shops.

∾

Must admit, I think, a fatal attraction to dissonance. It is like my attraction to contrast in photography. I am intellectually and emotionally, but not visually, engaged by the subtle modulations of gray.

∾

Clown couple ties the knot.
Dow Jones stocks start the day in positive territory.

AUGUST 22

Breakfast at Georgian Room. French toast as gooey and decadent as we remembered. Spent most of the day at Pike Street Market. Emily bought Xmas presents for the family (hippie-made candles of medieval design). Gelato over on Third, of course. Picnic under the Henry Moore sculpture on Spring St. (sandwiches from Three Girls Bakery).

∾

Spontaneous goat manure fire stinks up Vt. town.
21 measles cases linked to megachurch in Texas.

AUGUST 23

Hike along the waterfront. Scarf shopping downtown. Birthday dinner at The Pink Door. Dined on the patio overlooking the bay. Gust of wind. Me (not the rigatoni) dusted in freshly grated parmesan.

∾

Mercury contaminations in fish to double by 2050.
Couple married 65 years die 11 hours apart.

AUGUST 24

Took train home. Found a present on the front porch—a fruit basket from Lewis and Leah. Gobbled down a half-dozen chocolate-covered strawberries and made myself sick.

∾

Tropical storm Fernando heads toward Mexico's coast.
Sharp fall in orders for durable goods.

AUGUST 25

Light rain. Work.

∾

When was the last time I read the warning label on a package of anything?

∾

New telescope will be 10 times sharper than Hubble.
Truck crash blocks I-84 near The Dalles.

AUGUST 26

New review of chamber piece. Very nice. Lovely job of summation, of sorting the unsortable. In closing, the reviewer expressed a preference for another one of my compositions: String Quartet in C minor. Think it is the one that Emily prefers as well.

∾

I get the feeling Christine is perplexed by (and disapproving of) my middle-classness. People like me, people in the arts, are supposed to be either very rich or very poor. My in-betweenness disrupts her interpretation: artists are either recognized and lavishly rewarded or unrecognized and destitute.

∾

Broadway star dies at 87.
US Treasury to reach "debt limit" by mid-October.

AUGUST 27

Downtown. Captured pretty good photo of alfresco ballet class. Also, pretty good shot of guy in fedora manning the take-away window of Floyd's Coffee Shop.

∾

Balderdash ran in his first race yesterday. He did not do very well, but Whately still excited. Had a small party with other owners in celebration. Devolved from a dinner thing into a drinks-and-poker thing. Lost another fistful of his real-estate money. Seems unfazed.

∾

Britain recalls Parliament to discuss Syria.
Conn. officer kills lizard menacing chickens.

AUGUST 28

Reading last night about delusional people—people who believe they have some sort of "special" power. These beliefs can cause all sorts of problems, of course, but they must have their compensations. The pleasure of feeling exceptional, for instance.

∾

Bear attacks on the rise.
Scientists say existence of new element confirmed.

AUGUST 29

Eye exam. Everything good. No change in my prescription.

∾

Had new piano tuner in. Walter Something. Once a professional—now hard times. From what I could tell, life for him seems to revolve around prescription painkillers and war with his hairline.

∾

Iran to work with Russia to stop strike on Syria.
2 arrested in April assault on Timbers fan.

AUGUST 30

Lunch with Emily. Ham sandwiches. Picked up newspaper and 12 bars of soap.

∾

Do not know anyone with a nickname. Proof—if any needed—that I have led (and am leading) a sheltered life.

∾

Albany couple arrested in death of daughter, 12.
Loose kittens halt largest US subway system.

AUGUST 31

Wandered through art festival in the Pearl. Up-market schlock mostly. Lunch at the bakery, then over to Powell's. Picked up a new novel and a book about Washington, D.C.

∾

Had Emily listen to first draft of fugue. She said she liked it, but she pretty much always says that. To me it seemed a waste of time. Will probably give it a light combing and toss it in a drawer.

∾

Note to Self: Worry less.

∾

Seamus Heaney, Irish poet, dies at 74.
Yankees 2, Orioles 0.

September

SEPTEMBER 1

Movie. Latest from doddering comic auteur. Best thing he's done in a while. Not exciting, but at least, for a change, not annoying.

Reading experimental novel of some acclaim. Text and photos are promiscuously mingled. One of these photos is of a foreign-ish family—a group of four. The father stands comfortably at the center. Wife, son, and daughter are squeezed in right and left. The father's garishly patterned shirt (a salad mix of rhombuses and hexagons) is partially unbuttoned showing a great V of hairy chest. It's like a woman with an unbuttoned blouse showing you a generous helping of breast. His manliness—it is the first thing he wants you to know about him.

Request from internet reviewer for copy of latest score.

~

Idaho lady dislocates shoulder at Ore. rodeo.
Seattle police arrest man with loaded crossbow.

SEPTEMBER 2

Grocery store. Yard work. Pizza.

∾

The Bennett's daughter Clare is getting married. Everyone is excited, but also a little nervous. The wedding is going to be in Chicago where the groom (a numbers-fiddler of some sort) and his family live. Clare will be moving there. The city frightens her. She has never lived anywhere but here with her parents.

∾

Concert. Emerson Auditorium. Heard Baldwin Quartet playing a pair of familiar Beethoven pieces. Approach was restrained—perhaps a little too much so. Felt deference was more to the demands of the performance than to the sophistication of the score.

∾

Clouds moving into metro area for Labor Day.
Zoo tries to pass off dog as lion.

SEPTEMBER 3

The November show "Town and Country" arrived today. Fifteen images printed and framed. Spent an hour unpacking and inspecting. Each piece bubble-wrapped, bubble-wrapped, and bubble-wrapped again—like a Ming vase. At first glance they look pretty good. Just what I wanted for the venue—simple, conservative stuff, but strong. Only one image a bit of a disappointment—a picture of a ramshackle gallery on the coast. It's 8x12. Needed to be bigger to work. Wait for Emily to have a look and then, with some effort, back in the boxes ready for transport Nov 1.

∾

Janet cancelled Saturday's dinner date. Mysterious medical necessity. Can't eat (or drink) anything interesting for the next three weeks.

∾

Israel and US conduct missile test in Mediterranean.
Woman found dead in backyard pool.

SEPTEMBER 4

Beth, my haircutter, is one of those people who wants to seem not just good, but quintessentially good; not just sensitive, but hypersensitively sensitive. The sort of person who on a bad day seeks the counsel of white witches and acupuncturists, who talks of shamans the way a five-year old talks of Santa. Her place is filled with fine feeling, the taste of scented candles, and the oppressive aura of her miserable little dog, Norman.

∾

Ex-teacher may face more prison time for rape.
Sellwood Bridge interchange snarls traffic.

SEPTEMBER 5

Phillip McGann, friend of a friend, died two days ago. He left instructions—said he wanted one-half of his ashes scattered in the ocean, the other half some place in Ireland. Always indicative to me of a peculiar, religious relationship to the idea of death, these sorts of instructions. If I am dead, what possible difference could it make to me where the physical remains of my body are deposited? The idea may have provided some anomalous sort of comfort before I died, but once I'm gone, scatter the ashes on a favorite beach in the Bahamas or keep them in a cigar box in the garage—it's all the same to me.

Talked for a while with Christine about photography. Showed her a shot I had taken and was about to discard for technical reasons. I have been advised by many that such concerns are pedestrian—still, these types of imperfections bother me. I can think of only one photo I have kept that has not met a sort of minimum standard: a juggler.

Landscapers working across the street along with the construction people—so leaf blowers, hedge trimmers, lawn mowers along with hammering, sawing, and hollering.

Lost python found in Tigard neighborhood.
Man fills home with 6,000 Barbie dolls.

SEPTEMBER 6

NFL season opened last night. Denver Broncos vs. Baltimore Ravens. Broncos behind at half-time when the quarterback took over and became the sixth man in NFL history to throw seven touchdown passes in a game. Was last done in 1969.

∾

Trying to move on in a new acclaimed novel I started reading the other night, but having trouble. The thing is padded with a lot of not-very-good writerly writing. Feel the author has had his eye on the word count, that his publisher (or agent) has provided specifications.

∾

Hitler's WWII bodyguard dies at 96.
Sinkhole swallows car in Oklahoma City.

SEPTEMBER 7

Urban hike, Emily and I. Discovered remarkable glass sculptor at Bullseye. Best show we have seen there in years. Stopped later at Powell's. Picked up a book of Bill Brandt's photographs. Had lunch at new place over near the Everett Street Bistro. Good, but menu limited.

∾

Received proof copy of promo calendar. Making a few changes. Different cover, different paper, replacing one image inside (March).

∾

IOC wants cyclist to return Olympic medal.
Largest Ferris wheel nears completion in Las Vegas.

SEPTEMBER 8

Sunday football. Not as much fun as it could have been because our refrigerator died—or, more accurately, because we thought our refrigerator died. Spent an hour trying to schedule a repair man, which is something you pretty much can't do on a Sunday. Discovered later in the day that the refrigerator was actually fine, that someone (probably me) had not gotten the door to the freezer closed the last time they were in it. It was this unclosed door that caused the costly thaw. All temps are now back where they should be. Half a day and several pounds of ham ruined.

∾

Cat survives 11-story fall from Alaska apartment.
Long-lost Van Gogh painting identified.

SEPTEMBER 9

Another encounter at the mailboxes with Mrs. Hampton. The subject today was bees. She has been reading up on anaphylactic shock. She thinks if she is stung by a bee, she will die.

∾

Note to self: Check expiration date on Paris Review subscription.

∾

Assad says U.S. strike would bring "repercussions."
New wife charged with pushing husband off cliff.

SEPTEMBER 10

Bad night's sleep. Up since 4:00 a.m. with aimless thoughts of death, dying, and disability.

∾

Lunch with Holly at West Union Pub. Wish it had better food. They serve breakfast until 1:00 so ordered an egg scramble in the hope that such an easy thing would be edible. It almost was. Nice to catch up. Been a while. She has a new dog, a boxer named Lucy.

∾

Syria agrees with plan to destroy chemical weapons.
Koch to buy Molex for $7.2 billion.

SEPTEMBER 11

An unusual 90+ degree day. I am never happy to see one. It is, I think, a new record for the date.

∾

Reading book on the photographer Paul Strand. Knew nothing about him. Disheartened to discover he spent much of his creative life making films—the "videos" of his day. After ten years of this, he retreated at age 53 back to still photography.

∾

Somber tributes mark 9/11 anniversary.
FDA announces new labeling and safety rules for opioids.

SEPTEMBER 12

Man finally showed up to paint our fence. Short, bespectacled, muscular, loud, and by some standards (but not mine) meticulous. The Homeowners' Association has been dragging its feet for all sorts of reasons—most involving the ongoing but almost-over lawsuit. This painting is something that should have been done a year and a half ago.

∾

If I tried, how many presidents could I name?

∾

Miss America contestant shows off tattoos.
1400-ton molasses spill killing thousands of fish.

SEPTEMBER 13

Erin, a friend of Emily's, had her car broken into last night. Nothing was stolen because there was nothing to steal, but the passenger-side window will have to be replaced. She seems to have taken the incident in stride—accepted it as part of the price she pays for living where she lives. A sort of nuisance tax on city slickers.

∾

Brief talk with editor Boyle. *Left Coast* will not be paying me quite as much as they were for a piece. The money is being reallocated—invested in higher-profile work (phosphorescent stories of the substance-abusing rich). Not happy, but not particularly upset. Wasn't much more than a token payment to begin with. I have no illusions about my place in the grand scheme of things here.

∾

Russian shot in quarrel over Kant's philosophy.
37 dead in fire at psychiatric hospital.

SEPTEMBER 14

Out to Sellwood for an amble among the antique shops. Favorite place is called The 1875 House. It is filled with amazing stuff, more still-life subjects per square foot than any other place in town.

∾

Lunch at Grand Central Bakery.

∾

Talked with Jim Hammond about a federal investigation into the campaign shenanigans of an ambitious Republican governor. He told me he couldn't be less interested. Understood completely.

∾

Phillip Levine is awarded $100,000 poetry prize.
Deadly amoeba found in Louisiana water supply.

SEPTEMBER 15

Football, football, football. Lots of good games. Lots of lumpish lolling on the couch. It's early in the season so not yet quite in shape for extended periods of sedentary mindlessness.

∾

Powerball jackpot swells to $400 million.
Lightning strikes tree in Aloha as storm moves through metro area.

SEPTEMBER 16

Met with Christine. We talked a bit about our last visit, about some things I had said about a certain literary lion. She was, I think, giving me a chance to amend some of those comments that had been indiscreetly negative.

∾

Boston homeless man turns in money-filled backpack.
Powerful typhoon lashes Japan.

SEPTEMBER 17

Thinking of writing a part in my next piece for the bassoon just to see if I can. I am not, on the whole, in favor of such exercises (too much about ego, too little about art), but this would be just for me. Think of it as a ridiculous instrument, an oboe with a cold.

∾

What is that tumbling around in the dryer?

∾

Gunman and 12 victims killed in shooting at D.C. Navy Yard.
Students accused of cheating return to Harvard.

SEPTEMBER 18

Emily had an MRI on her back today. Step one in sorting out what is very likely to be a significant problem. See doctor for an interpretation of the findings week after next.

∾

Ran into Bob and his ugly, rust-colored dog, Ed. He, Bob, is a retired teacher with heart problems. For a year or so he has been asking me to read the memoir he is working on. It is the story of his calamitous childhood, of growing up somewhere in the Midwest, I think.

∾

Hood River bank robbery suspect captured.
Researchers discover source of imagination in human brain.

SEPTEMBER 19

Dodd has been experimenting with a pipe. Not a good idea. Seems nothing more than a sad affectation.

∾

Made a few tweaks in the financial arrangements with the cafe where I am hanging show in November.

∾

Ant attack kills Texas football player.
Study: red wine, blueberries may boost your immune system.

SEPTEMBER 20

Working on a new piece. Playing again with structure and with conventional harmonic progression. Semblance of tonality retained.

∾

University and faculty union agree on 2-year contract.
Pa. man on riding lawn mower charged with DUI.

SEPTEMBER 21

Emily saw Clare at her haircut place this morning. She asked her about the wedding plans. Clare said she was nervous, more nervous than she thought was normal under the circumstances. She is thinking about getting professional help—a prescription that will make getting married possible.

~

Texas inmate blows kisses before execution.
New species of legless lizard discovered in Bakersfield.

SEPTEMBER 22

Rain and cold. First day back lounging in beloved sweatpants. Watched Green Bay's excruciating loss to Cincinnati. Annoying game.

~

Note to self: Look into latest recommendations vis-a-vis Vitamin C.

~

Kenya moves to end mall siege as death toll rises to 68.
Doctors working to develop breast-cancer vaccine.

SEPTEMBER 23

Going through a difficult period. Having a hard time caring about what I am doing—about my music and my picture-taking. Am putting together notes for another septet, but they aren't much. Have rough draft of a short semi-serialist piece I keep intending to get back to, but don't. As for pictures—it seems like a long time since I have taken a good one.

~

Germany's Chancellor wins third term.
Burger King launching lower calorie french fry.

SEPTEMBER 24

Reading latest novel in a series dedicated to illumination of generational zeitgeist. Remarkable moments of glumness. Am always amazed when I find in print someone more cynical than me.

∾

99-year-old Iowa woman gets high school diploma.
Second Bend fire started by electrocuted squirrel.

SEPTEMBER 25

Off to spend three days in Cannon Beach. Drive through farmland and forest is familiar and beautiful.

∾

Our regular hotel is under new management—professionally nice, but nothing more. Not used to feeling like strangers here. Cathleen, who we knew for years and who always went out of her way to make us feel welcome, has left to be with her ailing daughter on the East Coast.

∾

Egyptian police raid Islamist stronghold near Cairo.
NY girl gets trapped inside sofa bed, dies.

SEPTEMBER 26

Breakfast at Lazy Susan, as always. Favorite omelet and gingerbread waffle. Yasmine very pregnant. Due any day now. It's a girl. Two names: the first unfathomable, the second—the one by which she will be known—Isabella. Spent the day roaming up and down the beach. Ice cream for lunch, sandwiches and piece of pie from Sweet Basil's for dinner.

∾

NY snake salesman opens store.
City says "no" to church's planned potluck.

SEPTEMBER 27

First in a series of powerful storms arrived on schedule. Spent most of the day in town looking through shops. Amazing the amount of trinkety crap for sale here.

∾

Glitches expected for health law rollout.
Duck boat catches fire with 30 aboard.

SEPTEMBER 28

Drove home in heavy rain—Emily reading to me the whole way bits and pieces from the *Times*.

∾

Fatal car bombings rip Baghdad.
Judge hears claims that BP lied to Feds about oil spill.

SEPTEMBER 29

Grueling game between Seahawks and Houston. Seahawks, after being down 20 to 3, came back to win in overtime.

∾

Second part of storm system came through today with high winds and rain. Set new record. Wettest September since 1870 something.

∾

Seawater bacteria leaves 9 people dead.
Titan's Jake Locker out 4-to-8 weeks with hip injury.

SEPTEMBER 30

More storms. Schizophrenic system. Patches of sun and blue, then suddenly gullywashers.

∾

Back to work on old quartet. It has a better chance of being worth something than the one I just wrote, but I don't have a lot of hope for it.

∾

The Bennetts took Clare to the airport. She started hyperventilating and refused to get on the plane.

∾

Note to self: Be more enthusiastic.

∾

Federal government headed for shutdown.
Portland mom raises money for cancer study.

October

OCTOBER 1

Emily went to our quasi-autistic knee doctor for a check-up. She wanted an assessment of both her replaced knee (right) and non-replaced knee (left). Reports were all good. Big doctor visit will be on Thursday. We will hear news about the scan of her back. Neither of us expects this news to be good.

New print arrived from Massachusetts lab—a picture taken in an antique shop of a crowded corner filled with oil-burning lanterns. I like the evocation of time past and the representation of abundance. The first seems a primal theme for me, the second a metaphorical allusion to a metaphysical proposition.

Senate rejects latest House proposal.
5 hikers killed by Colo. rock slide.

OCTOBER 2

Have been reading a book about Washington, D.C.—about how it actually works, about turning power (who you know) into money and money into power. Am calling it quits at page 163.

∾

What is the difference, if any, between a convulsion and a seizure?

∾

Burglars ransack deli, get nothing.
Federal employees rally in downtown Portland.

OCTOBER 3

Tense and nervous meeting with Emily's back doctor for diagnosis of latest trouble and interpretation of scan results. Surgery, it seems, will be required, but both of us greatly relieved to find the problem, though serious, did not appear to be as catastrophically serious as we had feared in our gloomier moments. (Because of her family history we were expecting the assessment of her present condition to be bleaker and the forecast for her future to be less hopeful.) The plan is to fuse a pair of vertebrae in her lower back. Will probably have it done in February or March. Celebrated with a special bottle of wine—happy that we were not unhappier, that the bad news was not worse.

∾

Russian charge 14 Greenpeace activists with piracy.
Cornell Farm offers pumpkin painting workshop.

OCTOBER 4

Boyle is one of those people who likes to get telephone calls. They make him feel important. I am just the opposite—one of those people who does *not* like to get telephone calls. The fewer I get, the better—the less harried, distracted, and consequently depressed I feel. He is not sure what to think of me. My lack of worldly ambition makes him suspicious—inclines him to question my value.

∾

Note to self: Look into all-weather tires.

∾

Naked man tackled by police on I-405.
U.S. and Japan agree to broaden military alliance.

OCTOBER 5

Movie. Light comedy. Charming. Inconsequential. Cruised the galleries. Bought old exhibition catalogues from Blue Sky.

∾

Am thinking of developing a secret vice—something I could struggle heroically against from time to time but rationalize a capitulation to in the end as evidence of simple humanness.

∾

Italy suspends search for shipwreck victims.
New York Opera files for bankruptcy.

OCTOBER 6

Usual Sunday this time of year: football, exercise, grocery shopping, walk, work, television, wine, reading, grooming, putting the garbage out.

∾

Suspect carjacks man in Happy Valley at knifepoint.
Spanish shepherds guide 2,000 sheep through Madrid.

OCTOBER 7

Short piece of counterpoint going nowhere.

∾

Still reading early collection of Amelia Michaels' essays. My admiration for her borders on the idolatrous so I don't like finding problems with her work, but I have found one—a big one: her admiration of the giant horse's ass James Warrant. There must be a personal relationship. Something has clouded her critical judgment. Warrant is, without question, articulate and without question he has interesting things to say, but he is also without question an arrogant shoveler of polysyllabic shineola.

∾

1 dead 12 injured in shootout at Calif. dance.
Woman mauled by tiger at exotic animal park.

OCTOBER 8

Haircut. Beth her usual skinny self—full of complaints about dismissive daughter, sad enthusiasms for the mundane, and maudlin pronouncements on the wonders of nature. (Today it was the return of the swifts.)

~

The hammering across the street continues as repairs to the 30-some homes in that development inch along.

~

Towering tree falls on house in Hillsboro.
New $100 bills start circulating today.

OCTOBER 9

Received note from James Cook about writing a music review for the newspaper's new digital incarnation. We'll see. Have mixed feelings. Not that interested in doing it, but could be a welcome distraction from CQ.

~

Mrs. Hampton thinks she has a gas leak. She had the gas company out to inspect. They found nothing, but she is not convinced.

~

Downtown for lunch. Ran into Michael Epps. Michael has been making his living for a while now doing pet portraits, but he is restless. He sees himself as a more adventurous sort and is considering a foray into crime photography (and, down the road, war photography). He has made plans with a friend to go to a high-school football game next Friday. Washington vs. Taft. They are notoriously fractious rivals. There is always a significant and portending police presence.

∾

Salem homeowner, 82, shoots burglary suspect.
Foster Farms chicken tied to NW salmonella outbreak.

OCTOBER 10

Another review on the internet of my latest piece. Lovely, but not, unfortunately, hyperbolic.

∾

House cleaning. Monotonous bore. Changed bag in the vacuum cleaner and discovered (to my surprise) it was something I should have done a long time ago.

∾

Thomas Foster, glazed professional, ambitious smoozer, chief cheese of the Northwest Literary Alliance for the past five years, is establishing a fund to finance a literary festival and has invited me (via email) to make a contribution.

∾

Note to self: Be more flexible.

∾

Passengers stuck on Florida roller coaster.
Alice Munro wins Nobel for literature.

OCTOBER 11

Thinking again about doing an essay on the subject of artists' statements. I can't ever remember coming across one I liked, one that didn't make me dislike (at least a little) the artist writing it. These statements tend to be little more than pretentious sales pitches—efforts aimed at convincing you of an artist's enduring genius and of a price tag's astonishing modesty.

∾

City council aims to make Barber Blvd. safer.
Scott Carpenter, one of the original seven astronauts, dead at 88.

OCTOBER 12

Farmers Market. Seemed especially large and beautiful today—the fruit, vegetable, and flower stands each a work of art.

∾

Saw rock-n-roll legend in concert. Still has remarkable voice. Hard time with the crowd, as always. It's not so bad when we are seated and I am distracted by the entertainment, but the lobby during intermission is for me a hellscape.

∾

Cyclone lashes India's eastern coastline.
3 dogs missing after fire destroys NE Portland home.

OCTOBER 13

Exercise, football, grocery shopping. Seahawks win, but not as impressively as I would have liked. Torturous mix of extraordinary play and sloppiness.

∾

Christine has been looking into my music. Hope she can appreciate it to some degree for what it is—that she can suspend temporarily her bias in favor of conventional organization, that she will be open to the oblique theme, to the eccentric tonal study.

∾

Red Cross workers kidnapped in Syria.
Ancient DNA reveals Europe's genetic diversity.

OCTOBER 14

Columbus Day. Emily off. Spent a few hours wandering up and down 23rd Ave. Lunch at Papa Haydn's. We do this—eat there—about every three or four years. Always the same experience. Expensive, good but not great, service lousy. Never understood the place's enduring popularity. Known for their desserts, but these are mostly elaborate cakes—cakes I have no interest in.

∾

Belgians nab Somali pirate leader.
China earmarks millions to fight air pollution.

OCTOBER 15

Finished very, very, very rough draft of etude. Not promising. Will toss it in a drawer for a couple of days, then take another look.

∾

Met Conroy for lunch today at a place he recently discovered. Didn't recognize the name, but the table settings looked familiar. Think I have been there before. Can't remember when or with whom. The harder I try to remember, the less likely it seems I will.

∾

Two earthquakes rattle Bay area.
Museum seeks return of ancient gold tablet.

OCTOBER 16

When it comes to flamboyance I'm an Aristotelian. I interpret it as spectacle—the lowest form of drama. It is, in this day and age, the only form of drama anyone seems to have time for.

∾

18-foot-long sea creature found off Calif. coast.
Woman steals 80 lbs. of mail in Vancouver.

OCTOBER 17

The closer you look at the art scene the more it reminds you of the fashion scene. There is an obsession with what is currently in style, what is new, what is hot. The "movement" of the moment is just a way for hawking wares—the season's new color or neckline. These are not works of art, but works of commerce—status gewgaws.

∾

Congress votes to end 16-day shutdown.
Evidence suggests early Britons ate roasted toads.

OCTOBER 18

It is unfortunate but true—I have no interest in collaborative activities like making movies. I am attracted to the solitary pursuits—to composing, to writing, to painting, to photography.

∾

Convicted murderers mistakenly released from Florida prison.
Google stock hits record high.

OCTOBER 19

Emily had her hair done this morning, so late start on our Saturday adventures. Walked downtown along the river, lunched at a new Italian place in the Pearl, a visit to Powell's, and then to the art museum to see new show—a sprawling exhibition of Samurai armor.

∾

Epps and friend were assaulted at the football game last night. As expected, fighting broke out as gangs of Washington supporters (who lost) sought to even things up by attacking gangs of Taft supporters. Epps was taking pictures and was mistaken in the melee for some sort of law enforcement. He was pushed around, knocked down, and hit in the face. Camera and one of his more expensive lenses busted.

∾

Argentine commuter train slams into station.
Cards blank Dodgers, advance to World Series.

OCTOBER 20

Scratching at hypothetical etude. Features clarinet—the most honest and unambitious of the woodwinds.

∾

Brief talk with Phillip Miller. He is one of those people who likes alcohol because under its influence he feels better about himself, more content with who he is.

∾

Work begins on Calif. bullet train.
Police investigate threats against Texas senator.

OCTOBER 21

Visited Epps, the adventurer. He invited me over to see his swollen face. Showed me the only picture he got from the fight at the football game. Was pretty good—two small brawlers baring their canines and viciously attacking one another.

∾

6-foot alligator tries to enter Wal-Mart.
Student, staffer dead in Nev. school shooting.

OCTOBER 22

Packing for three-day vacation in Sisters and Bend.

∾

Think Christine is having trouble forming her opinion of me. I live and work in the shadows. The picture she is pasting together is almost wholly from life. There are no other sources to reference—to bounce impressions and propositions off of.

∾

Evacuations as hurricane looms off coast.
Vietnam seizes 2.4 tons of smuggled elephant tusks.

OCTOBER 23

A little fog to begin with, but relaxing and uneventful drive to Sisters. Stretched legs at Detroit Lake. Checked into hotel. Wandered around town. Chicken quesadillas for dinner, ice cream cone for dessert.

∾

Jobs report disappoints.
Groom who halted wedding with bomb hoax jailed.

OCTOBER 24

Breakfast. Sweet-potato pancakes. White-haired waitress in bunchy polyester blouse—larger, older, and nicer than my grandmother. Visit to clock shop, then out to Camp Sherman for a hike along the Metolius River.

∾

Jerusalem mayor fights to hold seat in local vote.
Calif. dog loses eye in beating by burglar.

OCTOBER 25

Drove scenic Hwy 242 to the lava beds and the Dee Observatory. Love this area. Like a moonscape. Jagged black rocks to the horizon. Then on to Sahalie Falls. Lush emerald green grotto, raging water, rainbows.

∾

Brief chat with a guy who cleans the public bathrooms in Sisters. (Used to do it in Bend.) Slim, pleasant, happy, conscientious man with missing teeth and peculiar mustache.

∾

3 killed in medical helicopter crash.
Network puts sitcom on hiatus.

OCTOBER 26

Breakfast at The Depot. One of the best we have had in a long time. Blueberry pancakes, two-egg scramble with spinach added. Pleasant drive home. Stop at Rosie's in Mill City for a couple of her famous cranberry scones.

∾

Robotic surgery helping pancreatic cancer patients.
Poll finds Democrat poised for big win in New York race.

OCTOBER 27

The Sullivan's dog has died. Mixed feelings. Nice enough, but prolific shedder with an inclination to bark at any and every unexpected sound. They have framed a photograph and placed it on their fireplace mantle. Not a very good photograph.

∾

Tossed another novel aside—this one at page 91. Having a harder and harder time with contemporary fiction. I would suspect it was just me (old and jaded) if I hadn't heard so many similar complaints.

∾

Singer dead at 71.
Windows smashed at 2 Hillsboro businesses.

OCTOBER 28

Note from cafe owner. Looks like I will be hanging my show Wednesday morning.

∾

When was my last tetanus shot?

∾

For some reason it feels like it is time to re-read Faulkner. Something other than *As I Lay Dying*.

∾

Odor from chili processor a nuisance.
Missouri woman's pet monkey stolen in Colorado.

OCTOBER 29

Continue the drip, drip, drip of quartet writing—the accumulation of notes that will end up either shaping the thing or filling my garbage can.

∾

Franzen? My feelings are an even mix of admiration and annoyance. Am perturbed by his preening self-regard and dazzled by the concision of his perception. Can love and hate him in the same sentence.

∾

Libyan gunmen steal over $50 million from bank van.
Texas man survives being hit by lightning twice.

OCTOBER 30

Show hanging postponed a week as the current exhibitor is temporarily unable to do tear-down.

∾

Ran into Heather this afternoon. Good to see her and to hear the old gang was still together. She looked great. How did I get older and she did not? Did she make some iffy deal with the devil?

∾

Social Security benefits increase announced.
Artist's heirs accuse trusted dealer of fraud.

OCTOBER 31

Spent evening with Emily passing out chocolate to the kids in the neighborhood. Many more than last year. (Not raining for one thing.) Lots of princesses.

∾

Note to self: Be less distant.

∾

Red Sox win Series.
Scores of migrants dead in the Sahara.

November

NOVEMBER 1

Christine wanted to talk about the book I published (a collection of essays on music) and the local literary community—my place in it (or more accurately, my lack of a place in it). Told her that, as a rule, I was not much of a networking sort of person.

11 rescued after bus goes into Kan. creek.
Severed finger leads police to Ariz. theft suspect.

NOVEMBER 2

Movies again. As always, I am particular about my seat. It needs to be on the aisle and back a bit. My nearest neighbors will be quickly but rigorously assessed as potential sources of annoyance—the tall; the wide; the talkative; the odoriferous; the restless; the heavy feeders; the users of electronic devices people with children; people who, for some reason, you just don't like the look of, etc., etc.

∾

Gator found under escalator at Chicago airport.
Elderly woman dies in fall from Wash. beach bluff.

NOVEMBER 3

Emily has picked up stories of marital strife from down the street. Mrs. Rhodes, who we all know because she frequently wanders the neighborhood with petitions (save our drinking water, recall Senator So-and-So), has discovered Mr. Rhodes is again on the prowl. We do not know Mr. Rhodes very well because he does not seem to want to know us. I sympathize with the predilection, but it has irritated a number of our more gregarious residents.

∾

Note from Jim. Wants to set up dinner date. November 16 looks good.

∾

State police seek help in finding elk poacher.
M23 rebels call for cease-fire with Congo military.

NOVEMBER 4

When was the last time I saw a complex legal case explained cogently on the local news?

∾

Google invests $608 million in Finnish data center.
Trove of Nazi-looted art reportedly found in Munich apartment.

NOVEMBER 5

Hung show at cafe. Went up faster than I thought. Looks okay—but, of course, the venue leaves a lot to be desired.

∾

Woke up to rattling screech. G sharp.

∾

Fighting what I hope will be a little cold, but expect will not.

∾

Motorcycle recovered in Calif. 46 years after theft.
Nursing-home worker kills resident and self.

NOVEMBER 6

Listless lump with sore throat and low-grade fever. Not going to be getting much done.

∾

Read piece on poet Marianne Moore—an extended review of a new biography. Knew only her name. Rare—a poet as interesting to read as to read about. “Self reliant like the cat—/ that takes its prey to privacy,/ the mouse's limp tail hanging like a shoelace from its mouth."

∾

Bay area man set on fire; teen arrested.
Copy of Napoleon's will up for auction in Paris.

NOVEMBER 7

Spent most of the day blowing my nose and watching television.

∾

Thieves steal 160 sheep near UK town of Wool.
New Tyrannosaur discovered in Southern Utah.

NOVEMBER 8

Another contemporary novel tossed into the resell pile. When was the last time I made it past page 150 in this sort of thing?

∾

Note to self: Consider new glasses.

∾

Record typhoon slams into Philippines.
Arm severed at Seattle fortune cookie factory.

NOVEMBER 9

Downtown for a little getting-over-my-cold walk. Saw Barth show at the Fesseden Gallery. Have very conflicted feelings about this guy. He made his mark not as an artist, but as an "ethnic artist." Met him once. Struck me as a self-absorbed horse's ass. Much of the work was, as always, slapdash—tossed off. Not new paintings so much as new $5,000 bills.

~

Wash. moves to extend Boeing tax breaks.
13 killed in Indonesian chopper crash.

NOVEMBER 10

Exercise, grocery shopping, football.

~

The Rhodeses have been seeing a counselor. Mrs. Rhodes is unhappy because Mr. Rhodes does not seem to like her, and Mr. Rhodes does not seem to like her because she is unhappy. So far it seems to have been nothing but charges and counter-charges.

~

Woman killed by cougar at wildlife sanctuary.
Lung cancer on the rise in Beijing.

NOVEMBER 11

Christine says I am a difficult person to draw conclusions about. She likes me when we meet, but as the days intervene between these meetings she becomes suspicious of her reaction. The first part of every new encounter is spent recapturing her positive feelings.

~

Re-paving work finishes on busy West Burnside.
Polio vaccination campaign in Sudan has failed.

NOVEMBER 12

Electrician in to replace ventilation fan in master bath.

~

Haircut. Beth's perpetually problematic daughter is ill and almost certain to miss an exam that would have been her last. Her graduation from high school (already pushed back) will be pushed back again.

~

Note to self: Look into new breakfast cereal.

~

Oklahoma senator's son killed in plane crash.
Iranian foreign minister blames West for snag in nuclear talks.

NOVEMBER 13

Another solicitation from Mr. Foster. The Northwest Literary Alliance is turning 25 next month. It is a reason to celebrate and apparently to fund-raise.

~

Body of ex-Brazil pres. being exhumed in probe.
Painting by Francis Bacon sells for world record $142m.

NOVEMBER 14

Just received a congratulations notice. My latest quartet was chosen as a finalist for a small music award. Nice surprise. It is not much of an award as awards go, but it is better than the proverbial poke in the eye with a sharp stick. Other works in the category were from big shots—from Grove, Straus, and Austin.

∾

Secret Service agents kicked off President's security team.
Prince Charles turns 65.

NOVEMBER 15

Mrs. Hampton is worried about the weather forecast. She is afraid she will be snowed in and run out of food.

∾

Had cable people in to set up a newer and faster something. What a nightmare.

∾

Opium harvest at record high despite efforts.
Kangaroo gets loose causes stir in West Texas.

NOVEMBER 16

Emily woke up with a cold.

∾

Computer guru over to fix the mess the cable guy left us with. No go. Looks like a bad piece of equipment. Will be cybernetically hobbled until next Thursday.

∾

FDA approves nerve stimulator implant for epilepsy.
China to ease one-child policy, report says.

NOVEMBER 17

Football. Grocery shopping.

∾

Do I dream more or less frequently than average?

∾

Thinking about my exhibition. Disappointed. It is not as I had imagined. Seems too simple, too conventional. There are a number of good pictures in it, but there are also several prints that are basically just "pretty." I did this on purpose—editing with an eye to the venue—but if I ever have another chance I don't think I'll be making that mistake again.

∾

Missing mushroom picker located near Mt. Hood.
Lion kills lioness in front of Dallas Zoo visitors.

NOVEMBER 18

Emily home ill.

∾

Computer still pretty much useless. No internet since encounter with the cable technician.

∾

Seem to be working on another crude atonal satire of romanticism.

∾

Forest Grove man killed while trying to cross road in a wheelchair.
Congress and court weigh restraints on N.S.A. spying.

NOVEMBER 19

Headlight out on red car.

∾

Note to self: Cut back on carbohydrates.

∾

Gunman opens fire at Paris newspaper.
NASA launches robotic explorer to Mars.

NOVEMBER 20

Saw an article about E. Gilbert with subtitle: What happens after a composer sells more than 2 million copies? Am thinking about writing a short essay—my story. What happens after a composer sells fewer than 200 copies? The short answer, of course, is nothing happens.

∾

Bride jailed after biting groom at wedding.
Pesky Salem seagull put to death.

NOVEMBER 21

Emily is having lunch with Julien, who is in town with her California aura for just a day.

∾

Received note from Jim Cook at the newspaper congratulating me on the award nomination. Asked if I had a review I wanted to do.

∾

Missouri executes infamous serial killer.
Oregon unemployment rate falls to 5-year low.

NOVEMBER 22

Took car in to have the headlight replaced. Covered by warranty so no charge. Waited while the work was being done and fiddled with notes for a new piece. Not easy as there were at least three different cell-phone conversations going on in the waiting area. The service rep's name is Ronald, but he goes officially by Ronnie. He is my age. What does it tell me about him that he chooses to be known by a diminutive?

∾

50th anniversary of JFK assassination.
Hollywood daughter wins Miss Golden Globe.

NOVEMBER 23

Note from cafe. They want to keep the photo exhibition up through December.

∾

Dinner with Jim and Mia. Lots of talk about the generations—those before and those after. Also, cats and dogs.

∾

Volcanic eruption gives birth to new island.
Eating nuts associated with reduced death rate.

NOVEMBER 24

Grocery shopping. Thanksgiving supplies and, of course, pumpkin pie from Jacaiva.

∾

Boating club held another memorial outing for Nancy Bergeson, a federal defender who was murdered in her home four years ago. Emily knew and liked her. The case is unsolved. No suspects. No leads.

∾

Shark kills surfer on Australia's west coast.
Egypt expels Turkish envoy.

NOVEMBER 25

Downtown. Took photograph of young lady with an elaborate hairdo—a rat's nest teased up two-feet tall that was, she said, endangered by the wind. Also took picture of a sturdy young woman with pet rabbit.

∾

Amtrak train with 218 aboard derails in S.C.
Wal-Mart names new chief executive.

NOVEMBER 26

Had first of what should be four Thanksgiving dinners tonight.

∾

Emily reports the Rhodeses have put their house up for sale. Divorce is in the air.

∾

Big storm threatens holiday travel in the east.
Reduced food stamp benefits burden families.

NOVEMBER 27

At what post-processing point does a photograph lose its legitimacy, cross over from the actual to the conceptual, from capture to confabulation? How much alteration is acceptable? When does the thing stop being a photograph and become something else—some other sort of image?

∾

Climber survives 800-foot fall on Mt. Hood.
Judge signs off on airline merger.

NOVEMBER 28

Packing for trip to the coast.

∾

Has anyone in my family ever had gallbladder disease?

∾

U.S. spy accused of murder in Pakistan.
Dinosaur skeleton fetches $650,000 at auction.

NOVEMBER 29

Beautiful drive to Astoria. Room on the river. Dinner—crab quesadillas.

∾

Burglars hit 5 stores in Forest Grove.
Dog found under rubble 9 days after tornado.

NOVEMBER 30

Cannon Beach for gingerbread waffles, then back to Astoria to wander the streets. Spent an hour in Vintage Hardware—an incredible "salvage" shop. One of my favorite places on the coast.

∾

Anniversary dinner at the Urban Cafe. Halibut.

∾

Extra-good bottle of wine. Lots of large ships sliding by. Occasional blast from implacable fog horns.

∾

Note to self: Embrace impulse.

∾

Ore. Zoo's youngest elephant turns 1.
Police copter crashes into Glasgow pub.

December

DECEMBER 1

Wind. Lashing rains. Dinner in our room. Sandwiches and peach pie.

∾

Metro-North train derails in the Bronx.
Wage strikes planned in 100 cities.

DECEMBER 2

Drive home is uneventful. Threatened snow did not materialize.

∾

Finished plans for Xmas trip to San Diego with family. Logistical nightmare—hotels, dinners, breakfasts, rental cars, sights to see.

∾

Truck carrying dangerous radioactive material stolen in Mexico.
Exercise helps treat dementia patients.

DECEMBER 3

Stuck my nose in a new novel—but not for long. There is a common voice in so much contemporary work—the voice of graduate-studentry, a voice that speaks to a certain coveted demographic (one cherished by television advertisers), the voice of a professor's pet who seems to think of him or herself as forever 27.

Bolshoi dancer gets 6 years for acid attack on director.
Nuns abducted by rebels in Syria.

DECEMBER 4

Cold weather moving in. Forecast decorated with dire warnings.

Decided to scrap the essay I was working on for Jim Cook. It just doesn't work.

Ken Hunt bought a lot with a valley view. He is going to build his dream house there. He has been saving aggressively for some time now—much to the despair of his wife and kids who would have liked better vacations, better cars, better birthdays, better cuts of meat in their beef stew. Things have never really been bad for them, but they have never really been any better than just okay either.

~

Note to self: Turn water off to outside pipes.

~

Man killed in shark attack while fishing in Hawaii.
Las Vegas mall modeled on Istanbul's Grand Bazaar.

DECEMBER 5

New quartet creeps along its petty pace from day to day.

~

Tried to read the Michaels' essays on Freud and psychoanalysis, but I could only stick with them so long. The subject interested me once, but not now.

~

Judge poisoned by wife of 45 years.
Dozens of whales stranded in Florida waters.

DECEMBER 6

Three days of record low temperatures. Dusting of snow. More expected.

~

Is regret a good thing or a bad thing?

∾

Perpetually perplexed by the pusillanimity of Democrats.

∾

Nelson Mandela, South African icon, dies at 95.
Man in tank gets reckless driving ticket.

DECEMBER 7

Movies. So-so bio pic about a man with AIDS. Should have been a half-hour shorter. Lead actor not one of my favorites, but he did a decent job as an emaciated cowboy.

∾

Quick trip to the nursery for wreaths.

∾

Dungeness crab season opens Dec. 16.
FDA approves hepatitis C drug.

DECEMBER 8

13 degrees.

∾

Emily and I had one of those late-night state-of-the-relationship talks. Exhausting.

∾

Reindeer escapes from Santa at Colorado mall.
Okla. Satanists seek monument by statehouse steps.

DECEMBER 9

House smells of pine needles.

∾

Received proofs of Astoria photos. There are, I think, two candidates for the Massachusetts lab.

∾

Camas firefighter attacked by dogs.
New cockroach resistant to cold found in Manhattan.

DECEMBER 10

More snow this morning. Also, new review of the last chamber piece. Short, inconsequential, but nice enough.

∾

Mrs. Hampton thinks there is something wrong with the electrical wiring in her house, that certain circuits are in danger of overheating and causing a fire.

∾

Sewage system backs up at Wilsonville prison.
2 adults, 4 children missing in frigid mountains of Nevada.

DECEMBER 11

Picked up the essay I thought I had stopped working on and worked on it again. Nothing. Another morning wasted. Very frustrating. Someone needs to take this thing away from me.

∾

Hunt has started working with an architect. They were out the other day surveying when a neighbor wandered over and introduced himself. Hunt did not like the look of him. Suddenly it appears his plot and his plans don't seem quite so perfect.

∾

Figure skating champ out of Olympic games.
Mars Rover finds life-supporting chemicals.

DECEMBER 12

Today Christine wanted to talk about reputation. The fact that I did not really have one—did it bother me? No. Can't imagine having one. Suspect it would be inhibiting.

∾

Pope is *Time* magazine's Person of the Year.
House GOP gets behind budget agreement.

DECEMBER 13

Thumbing through the new *Harper's*. Am perplexed yet again by a small advertisement in the back for Dr. Winnifred Cutler's Athena Pheromones business. (The last "o" in the word "pheromones" is rendered in the shape of a heart.) It says 74% effective in increasing affection. Mix the elixir (there is a formula for men and one for women) with your perfume or your aftershave, and it makes you more attractive to the opposite sex. One happy customer, Victor, attests to a 30 to 40% increase in his confidence.

∾

Uncle of North Korean leader executed as traitor.
Precision Castparts to close Arizona plant.

DECEMBER 14

Movie. Brazenly bleak. Not good. Not bad.

∾

Tried again to read a story by one of my old favorites and could not do it. What has happened to her? Iowa, I think. She has been teaching there for too long. Her work has lost its vitality, its daring—the things that made it interesting. She is no longer who she was. Now she is just another one of them.

∾

China lands probe on the moon.
Elderly woman rescued from frozen pond.

DECEMBER 15

Out in the early AM shooting night pictures of flood-lit trees in nearby neighborhood. Tripod, manual focus, slow shutter speed. Haven't tried this sort of thing in a long time. Couple of decent shots. Fog not as thick as I had hoped.

∾

Football, exercise, grocery shopping.

∾

Acting great dies at 81.
Michelin recalls 1.2 million tires in US.

DECEMBER 16

Woke up with the Monongahela in my head. Don't know where it came from. Can't remember the last time I heard the word.

∾

22 dead as bus plunges off Philippine highway.
Pensions targeted in budget deal.

DECEMBER 17

Haircut. Beth's depressed Chihuahua there as always, catatonic in his little beige bed.

∾

Broken sewer leaks into Ash Creek.
Girl, 13, brain dead after routine tonsil surgery.

DECEMBER 18

Communiqué from Andrew Foster. A famous poet (swashbuckler topped with nimbus of flaxen curls) will be in town next week. RSVP if I would like to attend an informal lunch with the man. Seating for the event is limited.

∾

Note to self: Get copy of birth certificate.

∾

Man wounded in Salem gang shooting.
Russia to deploy new railway-based missile.

DECEMBER 19

Neighbors to the east are moving out. Will be interested to see who replaces them. They were ideal—silent, trustworthy, invisible.

∾

Houston hotel displays half-ton chocolate Santa.
Babies snoring linked to later behavior problems.

DECEMBER 20

Arrived in San Diego early afternoon. Rendezvoused with Lewis and Leah in the Gaslamp District for dinner.

∾

Semi overturns spilling holiday hams on I-85.
Fla. homeowners' group bans playing in the street.

DECEMBER 21

Breakfast at Cafe Fulford. Complicated, expensive, not especially good. Point Loma. Spanish Landing. Dropped into a hat shop near our hotel. Lewis bought a Stetson. Dinner with everyone at an Italian place.

∾

Brooklyn fire kills girl, 16.
Boy missing for months before police alerted.

DECEMBER 22

Balboa Park. Art Museum, Photography Museum, Automobile Museum. Dinner at Croce's. Warm fig salad. Ghirardelli's for ice cream. Made small contribution to yearly income of semi-skilled street magician.

∾

Team honors cheerleader turned soldier.
Bangladeshi factory owners charged in fire that killed 112.

DECEMBER 23

Coronado Island. U.S.S. Midway. Dinner at Asti's.

∾

Mogul sells island in San Juans for 8 million.
Ex-boyfriend pleads guilty in woman's murder.

DECEMBER 24

Mission Beach. Crystal Pier. Xmas dinner at Anthony's, which, we were unhappy to discover, is no longer the place it used to be.

∾

Dense fog advisory for Christmas morning.
Holiday sales down for third week.

DECEMBER 25

Breakfast at Hilton. Fly home.

∾

How many essays have I come across in the last year that opened in a hospital emergency room? Too many. Illness, injury, decrepitude, disability, death—it seems someone with an M.A. is always trying to look on the bright side of these things.

∾

New Jersey prepares to hike minimum wage.
Switzerland gives pardoned Russian oil tycoon a visa.

DECEMBER 26

Christine brought up the subject of production. Did I feel like I had written a little or a lot. Haven't really thought about it much. Would have to say "little." Started late. Throw most things away.

∾

Family of 3 displaced by Camas house fire.
Cruise ship stuck in ice.

DECEMBER 27

Movie. Disappointing serio-comic thing about con men. Long. Tonally inconsistent.

∾

Why in the early hours do I suddenly feel the need to re-read Flannery O'Connor? I think it has something to do with the clarity of her vision, the certainty of her ideal.

∾

Woman stabbed husband with ceramic squirrel.
Winter whale watch week begins in Oregon.

DECEMBER 28

Picked up photograph (woman on motorcycle) from framer. Looks good. Very pleased.

∾

Is my memory what it used to be?

∾

Fire crews pull cow from McMinnville pool.
2 peacekeepers killed in Sudan's south Darfur.

DECEMBER 29

Exercise, grocery shopping, football. Seahawks won division title.

∾

Read story about teenagers by a writer with two first names. Extraordinary. It wore me out. Couldn't have cared less about the goings on, but the writing was phosphorescent, magical. The characters alive on the page.

∾

Texas billionaire dies at 82.
Python strangles security guard at luxury hotel.

DECEMBER 30

Emily has a toothache, laryngitis, and the beginnings of a cold. Is not the way to start a new year.

∾

Hunt has a revised set of house plans—plans that take his would-be neighbors into account. They change the way the place is going to look and the expense of building it. It will mean another year of saving. I can't imagine Joan, Brandon, or Samantha will be happy to hear that.

∾

Rockets fired from Lebanon into northern Israel.
Ariz. woman accused of trying to poison children.

DECEMBER 31

Emily is home sick. Made her a vat of chicken soup.

∾

If your theory is interesting but your photograph is not, what do you have? Literature? Illustration? Art?

∾

Note to self: Worry less.

∾

Cruise ship passenger goes missing.
Handyman suspected in triple murder.

January

JANUARY 1

Took down Xmas decorations.

∾

Pruned evil rose bushes. Front and back.

∾

Building explodes in downtown Minneapolis.
Hawaiian woman with long last name gets new ID cards.

JANUARY 2

Trying to put finishing touches on photo book titled *Portland Journal*. Re-processing a few images. Penning brief intro comment.

∾

Note to self: Buy bug spray and lightbulbs.

∾

Wal-Mart recalls donkey meat in China.
Evergreen Airlines files for bankruptcy.

JANUARY 3

Emily home today with her cough syrup and her cold.

∾

Picked up show from cafe. Sold one picture. One more than I expected.

∾

Cancelled dinner tomorrow with Janet.

∾

Blast in Beirut kills 5.
Brain samples stolen from Indiana medical museum.

JANUARY 4

John Gray, the mystery man who lives down the street, has remained a stranger to all of us except, it seems, to Michael Lott. Mr. Gray has, as I understand it, a stutter and the retiring personality that comes with it. Michael is his lone connection to the world.

∾

Ex-mayor killed by train while chasing his runaway dog.
Small plane makes emergency landing on Bronx expressway.

JANUARY 5

Grocery shopping, exercise, and football. Playoff games.

∾

Christine says I am problematic. I answer questions, but I do not tell a story.

∾

African migrants protest in Israel.
U.S. icebreaker to help stranded ships.

JANUARY 6

Stuck my nose back in the O'Connor biography. Disconcerting to discover an ambitious careerist, to see how much she was a part of the literary industrial complex—that cozy consortium of agents, editors, reviewers, prize judges, retreat directors, fellowship administrators, and faculty chairmen.

∾

3 hurt in icy crash on Columbia Blvd.
Experts warn Jan. 6 most depressing day of year.

JANUARY 7

Another morning, another argument with the alarm clock.

∾

Pestered again today (as I am most days) by the sense that I have missed something obvious in an argument with myself and that, as a result, I am mistaken about something—something I hope is trivial, but might not be.

∾

Deadline to move Belmont goat herd extended.
Troops battle al-Qaida fighters near Baghdad.

JANUARY 8

House cleaning.

∾

Move Montreal trip to the end of September.

∾

Emily and I took the Mitchells to breakfast this morning and discovered that one of our favorite places (a place we have been going to for twenty years) has been sold to philistines. We are—at the moment anyway—inconsolable.

∾

Ex-beauty queen gunned down in robbery.
President pushes GOP on jobless benefits.

JANUARY 9

Met again with Dr. Harris to firm up plans for Emily's back surgery. He has unusual handshake. It does not require decoding.

∾

Abducted Swedish journalist released in Syria.
Utah mom to give birth to daughter's daughter.

JANUARY 10

Me and parties—we just don't mix. Have no interest in dazzling or being dazzled. Make an effort from time to time, but can never really respect myself in the morning.

∾

Looks like the real moving-in next door has begun. Not only is there a child, there is a dog. Presages problems. Saw furniture and a pair of large paintings. However nice these people may be, it seems their taste in pretty much everything is staggeringly bad.

∾

Ford raised quarterly dividend 25 percent.
Chemical spill in W. Va. river spurs closures.

JANUARY 11

Bought Montreal travel book and memoir of hyperactive Russian immigrant.

∾

Cat rescued after 3 winter days in Ohio drainpipe.
Egypt's top general eyes presidential run.

JANUARY 12

Grocery shopping. Exercise. Football (second set of divisional playoffs).

∾

Gray has opened up to Michael because he is an obvious neurotic. A pacer, a sweater, an insomniac—he has been in therapy his whole life. Thinks he has privileged access, that he understands the human condition.

∾

Giant panda leaves San Diego zoo for new life in China.
Southwest flight lands at wrong Missouri airport.

JANUARY 13

Nosing around in Russian's memoir. He appears to have a weakness for juvenile exaggeration.

∾

Note to self: Look into new shoes—both black and brown.

∾

Woman posing for photo falls from Calif. cliff.
Gunman in Portland strip club shot by patron.

JANUARY 14

Ran into Lisa Keegan and her unmanageable dog, Jake. She caught me up on her latest operations (cataracts and heart valve).

∾

Note from one of Mr. Foster's minions. The Alliance, it seems, is sponsoring a reading and a raffle.

∾

Retail data boosts US stocks.
French president brushes aside questions over secret affair.

JANUARY 15

Christine wanted to talk about one of my photographs, one that is framed and hangs in my office. It is an austere shot of a dilapidated art gallery in Cannon Beach—a falling-down place that looks haunted. It was shot in winter. The tree out front is a leafless skeleton.

∾

Caffeine may help memory.
Little leaguer sued by own coach.

JANUARY 16

To a child (and I think to the majority of adults) there is no more singularly amazing animal than the tiger. It stalks stealthily all imaginative lives.

∾

Pope fires 4 cardinals from Vatican bank.
Giant smog cloud chokes Beijing.

JANUARY 17

Back to Russian's memoir. He had a great-grandfather who was robbed of a fortune and murdered. I have a great-great one who was somehow related to the legendary frontiersman Daniel Boone.

∾

Doomsday cult member goes on trial for gas attack.
R&B singer pregnant with 1st child.

JANUARY 18

Looking into possibility of replacing oldest car. Mixed feelings. Would like an update, but not sure spending the money is a good idea.

∾

Birds. I have always understood an interest in them—have it myself—but I have never understood a significant commitment to them nor for that matter a serious commitment to any creature that was not firstly a mammal.

∾

Dinner with Jim and Mia.

∾

Girl, 4, fatally shoots boy, 4, at Detroit home.
Alaska flight to Portland diverted due to fog.

JANUARY 19

Seattle won conference playoff championship. Game was, as always, an ordeal to watch. Secured win in the last 20 seconds with an interception in the end zone.

∾

Flu season here, hospitalizations on the rise.
United Nations running out of food aid for Central African Republic.

JANUARY 20

Movies. Oscar winner overacting in interminable story about Osage County.

∾

Notified that one of my photographs has been selected for an exhibition next month in a show on portraiture at the Black Box Gallery. It is a picture of a wind-blown old lady with her hair in braids.

∾

2 dead in Omaha plant explosion.
Biologists monitor pilot whales off SW Florida.

JANUARY 21

Beth's trip with her new boyfriend has been postponed. Can't imagine spending two weeks with her. She is nice enough, but I have no idea who she actually is. I know only that she has spent a lifetime trying to be someone else.

∾

Pa. couple advertises home as "slightly haunted."
Pakistan bombs militant hideouts.

JANUARY 22

Computer problems again. More time wasted. More money wasted as well.

∾

After a long absence, back to the O'Connor bio. Discovered yet another thing I did not know: peacocks like figs. It is something we have in common—peacocks and I.

∾

Note to self: Look for the spare umbrella.

∾

29.6-carat blue diamond found in mine.
New dress code for doctors and nurses.

JANUARY 23

Rendezvous at the mailboxes with Mrs. Hampton. She wants to take a trip to Bend, but she is afraid she will get lost, that her car will break down and she will never be found.

∾

U.S. tourist killed by elephants.
5 arrested in decades-old heist case.

JANUARY 24

Have not talked to anyone today except Emily. That was a brief conversation on the phone around noon. I know this is the sort of thing that is supposed to worry me and that it doesn't is probably diagnostically significant (foretells a shorter lifespan than that of gregarious and loquacious counterparts)—but it doesn't.

∾

Giant squid caught off coast of Japan.
35 feared dead in Quebec retirement home fire.

JANUARY 25

Breakfast at Bijou's and a trip through the galleries.

∾

Christine wants to know about my childhood, about my mother and father. Have to tell her sorry, this is not a discussion we will be having.

∾

Bought new car. Exhausted. Rationalizations positively ingenious.

∾

Activists spray graffiti on Capt. Cook's house.
Thousands get free flu shots at Salem health fair.

JANUARY 26

Dinner with the Rossis cancelled. Barbara ill.

∾

Continue to read the O'Connor bio in bits and pieces. Am at a loss to explain my from-out-of-nowhere interest in the writer.

∾

Maine mom gives birth in driveway.
2 minor quakes shake Longview area.

JANUARY 27

New print of U.S. Bank building photo arrived. Borders on the generic, but will serve its decorative purpose I think.

∾

Michael believes Gray was at one time either incarcerated or institutionalized.

∾

Avalanches cut off residents of Alaskan town.
Vial of Pope John Paul II's blood stolen.

JANUARY 28

Agreed to do a review of an upcoming concert for Jim Cook. Don't really want to (not a task I am fond of), but I welcome any excuse to stop working on the quartet.

∾

Man plunges to death from London skyscraper.
Rare winter storm brings ice and snow to US south.

JANUARY 29

Emily spent the afternoon at the doctor's getting her regular checkup. Everything looked good. She came home, as always, with recommendations not just for herself, but for me. More Vitamin D, more Calcium.

∾

The Black Box Gallery has put up the February portrait show. It is, I think, uncommonly bad. Lots of very uninteresting pictures, lots of color, lots of kids. I am surprised my old lady in braids made the cut.

∾

Kidnapped Wash. girl calls 911 from trunk of car.
House passes farm bill preserving crop subsidies.

JANUARY 30

Ran into Stuart Lybeck, a distant friend of Gene's. He has distracting, caterpillar-like eyebrows that command attention. They do not look real, but more like something made with mohair in an arts & crafts class.

∾

Hundreds of pythons found in home.
North Korea nuclear reactor restarted.

JANUARY 31

Emily getting manicure—something she likes to do from time to time. I do not understand the attraction.

∾

Note to self: Be more cheerful.

∾

Gassy German cows blamed for barn explosion.
12 artists inducted into Musicians' Hall of Fame.

February

FEBRUARY 1

The woman who has been cutting Emily's hair for I don't know how many years was hospitalized with a brain aneurism. Recovery is going to take months. A serviceable temp must be hunted for—a craftsman who is philosophically compatible, one predisposed to understatement and classical design.

Boulder nearly destroys Italian farmhouse.
Catholic diocese to file for bankruptcy protection.

FEBRUARY 2

Big game day. Best defense vs. best offense. Supposed to be close, but it wasn't. Seattle won easily: 43 to 8. Celebrated with a nice bottle of wine.

Art collection of reclusive heiress unveiled.
Castaway claims he drifted 13 months in Pacific.

FEBRUARY 3

Forecast is for cold—for snow and ice at the end of the week just when we are heading to the beach.

∾

Trying to get into the habit of drinking vegetable juice. At this point I have not been successful.

∾

Concert. Newman Hall. Syphilitic Schubert's famous *Octet*. Easy to write about. Clarinetist Davidson especially adept.

∾

Murderer escapes Mich. prison, abducts woman.
Growth worries hammer US stocks.

FEBRUARY 4

Christine says I seem to have little, if any, ambition. I say this is not so. I obviously have quite a bit. It's just not what is generally recognized as ambition. For instance, my ambition for this new quartet is to finish it, not to find it an audience or an award.

∾

Diana Needham showed Emily a letter she is writing to her ex-therapist. She wants to be sure she has left him with a good impression.

∾

Note to self: Make dental appointment.

∾

Fla. woman, 81, arrested for feeding bears.
Farm bill effects will be felt far and wide.

FEBRUARY 5

Windy, dry, and very cold (in the teens).

∾

Interesting correspondence with publisher of first essay collection. They have joined forces with another press and are asking, I think, to re-acquire the rights to the book. Not sure I am interested in letting go of control again.

∾

Feds bust violent $500 million oxycodone ring.
Fire traps nine a mile deep in gold mine.

FEBRUARY 6

I have no idea what my smile looks like. What I produce in the mirror on demand is not it—at least I hope it isn't.

∾

Surprise. Boyle is moving on already, leaving *The Left Coast* for slicker, better-paying pastures. He will not be where he wants to be yet, but he will be on his way. I imagine a lot of insincere handshakes are being offered. Who will be replacing him?

∾

Bombings kill at least 32 in Iraqi capital.
Taliban claim capture of military dog in Afghanistan.

FEBRUARY 7

Snowed in. Made big breakfast—ham, eggs, cantaloupe, muffin. Moved dates for beach trip to the end of the month.

∾

Started work on concert review.

∾

Unrest spreads in Bosnia.
Cops blame drunk godmother for tot's accident.

FEBRUARY 8

Still snowed in. Hunted up boots and earflap hat. Took heroic hike around the pond. Ice storm due tonight.

∾

Minnesota orchestra returns after lockout.
NM ambulance hijacked with sleeping worker inside.

FEBRUARY 9

Slow thaw began this afternoon.

∾

Who, I wonder, takes up the bassoon. Is it something one wants to do from early on—for whatever reason—or is it where one goes when they fail at oboeing?

∾

Therapists are today's priests—listeners, holy men offering uptake inhibitors and absolution.

∾

Swiss vote to set limits on immigration.
Zoo kills giraffe, feeds carcass to lions.

FEBRUARY 10

Heard from friends in Denver that they are splitting up. They have been married for almost twenty years. Good people. Feel bad for both.

∾

Mrs. Hampton is going downtown tomorrow. She showed me her purse. It contains a small can of mace, a whistle, and a box of Band-Aids.

∾

Astronomers discover oldest star in the universe.
Gunman kills two at cathedral in Russia.

FEBRUARY 11

Almost everyone in Emily's office is ill. Think there might be a curse on the place.

~

White House welcomes French president.
Newlywed dies in Utah parachute accident.

FEBRUARY 12

The quartet has a saving grace: the time I spend thinking about it is time I do not spend thinking about death, disease, or Congress.

~

Note from Thomas Foster. He would like me to invest in the region's creative future.

~

Massive sinkhole swallows vintage Corvettes.
Polar bear dies after eating purse and coat.

FEBRUARY 13

Christine is one of those vigorous people who think there is no problem that diet, exercise, and a vitamin supplement can't cure.

~

Note to self: Renew passport.

∾

Cable giant to acquire rival.
Kentucky pipeline blast destroys three homes.

FEBRUARY 14

Finished Flannery O'Connor bio. Affected deeply by the difficulty of her last few years and her untimely death.

∾

Emily had a nice talk with Diana (who is working on another cunning letter to her ex-therapist). She explained that other issues aside, her real complaint about Jeremy had to do with an unwelcome metamorphosis. When they were married he was nonpolitical. He became a Republican—a rabid one. He wanted her to be one as well. That was not going to happen.

∾

Man-eating tiger stalks villagers in India.
California bill may put warning label on sugary drinks.

FEBRUARY 15

Dropped box of tax papers on our accountant.

∾

Another trip into the unknown—this time to a doll show. Visited with a couple who make teddy bears out of all sorts of fur (mink, seal, rabbit, muskrat, etc.)—an old man with a long white beard, who, when he talks, whistles loudly through a set of store-bought teeth, and his proud wife, the artist.

∾

Man posts ad seeking to buy 10-year old girl.
Volcano erupts in Indonesia.

FEBRUARY 16

Dinner with the Rossis at a place called The Woodsman. Trout and pork chops. Very good. Did some catching up. Not easy. The Rossis' lives are preternaturally complicated.

∾

Calif. wine-grape growers celebrate bumper crop.
Police hunt Venezuela opposition leader.

FEBRUARY 17

Lousy movie. American GIs rescuing art treasure in WWII.

∾

Massive asteroid to whiz past earth.
Camel escapes, attacks man in Southern California.

FEBRUARY 18

Using new lens on new camera to do an interior still-life sketch of home—a series I am calling (I think) "Notes from Home." Perhaps it should be "Still Home." Bookcase. Leather coat, etc., etc.

∾

Reading Teresa Wolfe. Brilliant. Relentlessly manipulative. Sociopathic narcissist dressed as spiritual innocent. No level on which she can be believed. Just when you think hating her might be too much, you realize it is not enough—that there is something more to her disagreeableness, that she is, in fact, evil. Her photo fascinates me. Too many teeth perhaps, but still the most average-looking woman. I cannot put her visage together with the malevolent spirit behind these essays. It's as if kind old Aunt Sally had written *Thus Spake Zarathustra*.

∾

Woman trapped under fallen tree escapes.
Dollar hits seven-week low against Euro.

FEBRUARY 19

Spent large part of lunch listening to Joseph Early unwrap his antediluvian theory of government.

∾

Finished a rough draft of the concert review. Unpleasant work. I'm not a salesman. Have no interest in arguing my opinions.

∾

25 killed, hundreds injured in Kiev clashes.
Race car museum breaks ground in Wilsonville.

FEBRUARY 20

Today's version of the writer's life is not one that appeals to me. Seems to be all about getting on stage as often as you can. Workshops, literary festivals, lecture series, bookstore readings, radio interviews, television interviews, magazine interviews—etc., etc., etc.

∾

Church floor collapses injuring dozens.
President apologizes to art history professor.

FEBRUARY 21

Haircut. Another half-hour of agonizing chit-chat with Beth.

∾

Christine is having a party. Emily and I are invited. I am, of course, reluctant. Her place will be filled to the fluted sconces with local big shots—the ones I try to avoid. Lots of up-market shoptalk.

∾

Note to self: Find gray sweater.

∾

Mystery arsonist terrifies plane passengers.
Kelso man found dead in flooded basement.

FEBRUARY 22

Saw Jim and his occasional band tonight at Donovan's. Old guys playing the rock-n-roll of my misspent youth. Loved it.

∾

Returned to Russian immigrant's memoir. Just started and already getting tired of him. Too much jumping up and down on the page, too much trying to make you marvel at his mind, too much trying to make you like him.

∾

Massive jade boulder found in Myanmar.
Coal-ash dumps threaten community.

FEBRUARY 23

We were going to the beach today, but Emily woke up with an abscessed tooth—her lip and face swollen. Couple of emergency calls got us a bottle of antibiotics. She sees dentist tomorrow morning.

∾

Scientists find oldest piece of earth.
Fifteen cases of measles confirmed in California.

FEBRUARY 24

Dental work in morning; beach in the late afternoon. Emily lopsided and big-lipped, but feeling much better.

∾

Bangkok blast kills three at protest zone.
US ambassador to Russia leaves troubled post.

FEBRUARY 25

Windy beach walk. Bought new novel by English experimentalist. Dinner at The Irish Table. Jumbo prawns. Wonderful as always.

∾

Leopard breaks into hospital, sparks panic.
Couple discovers $10M in gold coins while walking dog.

FEBRUARY 26

Breakfast at Lazy Susan, of course. Gingerbread waffle, of course. Long walk on beach, of course. Beautiful. Dry, sunny, still, mild—ideal. Found Emily a new coffee mug. Salmon tacos for dinner.

∾

Avalanche buries 2 snowmobilers.
Marathon spelling bee runs out of words.

FEBRUARY 27

Breakfast. Beach. Home.

∾

Supreme Court divided in climate case.
Man cleaning room finds $1M lotto ticket.

FEBRUARY 28

Gave up on yet another novel. Started it three times now and have never gotten past page 81. I can't read anything anymore.

∾

Diana showed Emily another letter to her ex-therapist. Said it was going to be her last, but Emily has doubts. (She describes Diana as "voluble.") Diana suggested the therapist had been biased in her husband Jeremy's favor and that this bias was, in all likelihood, the product of unconscious homosexual urges. She offered him some advice about how to better do his job.

∾

Note to self: Make peace with the unpredictable.

∾

Secret tunnel found under drug kingpin's bathtub.
Average gas prices jump 12 cents per gallon.

March

MARCH 1

Went on expedition to the southeast side of town for an open-studio event (sculptors, ceramic people, a painter or two), then to early dinner with Janet and her new boyfriend, Oliver.

∾

Russia approves use of military in the Ukraine.
Twins, 80, die working on antique car.

MARCH 2

Exercise, grocery shopping, walk downtown.

∾

Academy Awards tonight. New rules. Little interest now.

∾

Sent camera off to the manufacturer for repair of the shutter mechanism.

∾

North Korea fires two short-range missiles.
Vancouver man dies in single-car collision with tree.

MARCH 3

Heard from Dodd that Thomas Foster, president of the Northwest Literary Alliance, was rushed to the hospital last night. He died there at 4:15 this morning.

∾

Semi dumps apples in Hwy 97 rollover crash.
Powerful storm lashes eastern US.

MARCH 4

Community in shock about Foster. 47 years old. No intimations of mortality. Cascade of condolences.

∾

Scientists resurrect mysterious ancient virus.
Honor student booted from home, sues parents.

MARCH 5

I have lost some of my admiration for Cezanne. It seems to have happened without warning. I would like to feel about him the way I always have, but I don't. I still prefer him to most of the Impressionists, but I find him a little too comfortable now. I don't think it's simple familiarity, but it could be.

∾

Began work on old draft of short string piece titled *Satirist's Serenade*. Not sure it is worth it, but I suspect I will find out.

∾

Neither Emily nor I understand or revere money the way we should.

∾

Note to self: Replace furnace filter.

∾

13-year-old N.J. boy dies after dog attack.
Roommate arrested in Portland stabbing death.

MARCH 6

Christine wants to know if the lack of interest in my work has depressed me. The simple answer: No.

∾

Mrs. Hampton, I discover, is afraid of confined spaces—elevators in particular.

∾

Archbishop under fire for lavish home remodel.
Mich. woman found mummified inside car.

MARCH 7

Street shooting today. Usual miscellany—father with daughter riding on his shoulders, couple dancing in the square, man with shamrock-covered hat polishing a pair of shoes out in front of the library.

∾

The Bonds have had a fight. Charles has headed off to his parents' beach house. It's a small, rundown little thing on the outskirts of Manzanita. Cheryl is at home.

∾

Malaysia Airlines jet vanishes.
Calif. 3rd-graders caught smoking pot at school.

MARCH 8

Visit to the art museum. The most expensive painting in the world (at the moment anyway) is on display—a Bacon triptych of Lucian Freud in his studio. It's here until the end of the month (some sort of tax dodge) when it heads off to California or Las Vegas. Liked it but have never been much of a Bacon fan. In part I think it is his reliance on biomorphic forms. Simply does not appeal to me as a rule. Prefer hard lines of geometry. Took pictures of two expensively dressed art-ladies studying the thing.

∾

Daylight savings time. Spent half-hour turning back clocks.

∾

Egyptian journalists kept in cages during trial.
Fortune cookie turns Bronx woman into millionaire.

MARCH 9

Replaced floor plant in bedroom.

∾

Boyd is gone. There were a number of things I did not like about him (his complete lack of interest in what I was doing, for instance), but one thing in particular was his inclination to spend money (some of which came out of my fees) on the impressifying of his office. He knew it could not be grand, but he wanted it to be big. He wanted you to feel diminished on entry. He is being replaced by a man named Patrick Downs—at present an unknown quantity.

∾

Four new man-made gases threaten ozone.
Nuns kidnapped by Syrian rebels are freed.

MARCH 10

Lunch with Phillip and friend. Friend's first question on introduction was the first question I often get: am I a composer who takes photographs or a photographer who composes? The subject must be defined. I acquiesce by allowing that the former is perhaps the most accurate of descriptions, but caution that he should not underestimate my commitment to the latter.

∾

Pizza chain files for bankruptcy.
Body found in restroom at Vancouver mall.

MARCH 11

Met with financial people about account. Lots of papers to fill out, of course. Thoroughly unpleasant experience. Agent was officious, passive-aggressive, animatronic bureaucrat.

∾

Trolley bridge demolished, history gone.
Los Angeles man charged in severed head case.

MARCH 12

Landscapers have been through the neighborhood putting down a new layer of bark dust. The whole place now smells of cedar. Wonder if anyone in New York knows this aroma.

∾

Continuing work on quartet. Feels like I'm trying to fill a swimming pool with a soup spoon. Not quite sure why I am putting myself through this again.

∾

CIA accused of spying on Senate committee.
Death-row inmate to walk free after 30 years.

MARCH 13

Foster funeral. Felt like a literary event. Poobahs and power couples.

A measurable change in temperature when director Aaron Whittaker arrived. Lots of people introducing themselves. Would say that he and Anna Marshall (novelist who writes literary science fiction) are the two biggest fish in the local cultural pond.

Things have not been going well for Aaron lately. His last two movies were both critical and commercial flops. (He has an aide, Neal Byfield, who keeps an enemies list of people who say snide things about Aaron and/or his movies—snide things about his career being over.)

There are only two sets of people here who I know for certain are not important. They are the couples seated on either side of Emily and me.

Death toll rises in NYC building collapse.
FDA defends approval of controversial painkiller.

MARCH 14

One of the problems with attending funerals is that if you are not careful, you will come away trying to imagine your own and you will not be happy.

The bigness of death is the smallness of it. People suffer. They die by the thousands every hour. A match is struck in

Singapore, a porch light is turned off in St. Paul. Life is a cosmic twinkle.

∾

NY girl, 5, spends day at wrong school.
Portland unveils new eastside bikeway project.

MARCH 15

Movie. Slight, forgettable, Canadian.

∾

When is the last time I took anything apart?

∾

North Korea fires 10 short-range missiles.
Four feared dead in British helicopter crash.

MARCH 16

Christine complaining. Says we talk, but she still does not feel she is getting to know me.

∾

I have little interest in the art of artless photography, in the chance slapdashery of the vernacular or snapshot aesthetic. I do not find the thoughtless response quintessentially authentic or the considered image inherently flawed.

∾

Liver disease drug effective in trial.
Dannon to reduce sugar in yogurt for kids.

MARCH 17

Bond is a real-estate agent. I don't think he ever imagined himself as that. I think he imagined himself as someone interesting and well-off. He is neither. He just spent a week at his parent's beach house drinking and reassessing his life. Says he dreamed regularly of dying—mostly in automobile accidents, but occasionally it was by his own hand.

∾

Greenland ice melt accelerating.
Miss Congeniality cited in Chehalis for shoplifting.

MARCH 18

Conference with Emily's doctor. Everything suggests we have made the right decision. Surgery to fuse the lower part of her spine is scheduled for April 9.

∾

Earthquake rattles Los Angeles area.
Fashion designer uses scarf to hang herself from doorknob.

MARCH 19

Charles returned home with a story about meeting someone. He wanted to make Cheryl jealous. He confessed after a few questions that the story was not true. The troubles for them are, I think, just beginning.

~

Teen saves woman, 94, from burning home.
Gravitation waves offer new insight into Big Bang.

MARCH 20

Christine wanted to know if I thought there was any difference between my long-form compositions and my short. Answered yes. Long-form work is aimed at a broader narrow audience than the short.

~

Note to self: Return brown towels.

~

Rising food prices bite into household budgets.
TV show to profile late Alaskan serial killer.

MARCH 21

Emily will from time to time talk in her sleep. She does this less now than she used to. Me—this is not something I think I have ever done.

~

Crews try to contain spill in Galveston Bay.
Lawmakers attack cost of new hepatitis drug.

MARCH 22

Walked the eastside esplanade along the river. Beautiful day. Saturday Market. Cherry trees in bloom. Lunch at Huber's—turkey enchiladas.

∾

Woke up to a glistening hiss. B sharp.

∾

Washington mudslide kills three.
Elephants escape from circus, damage cars.

MARCH 23

The readiness of some people to believe almost anything they are told astonishes me. There are no skeptics in the world anymore. Everything is newer, better, or improved these days. Some sort of mercantile faith in the idea of progress has triumphed.

∾

Oregon exports stall.
New Jersey man drives van into backyard pool, dies.

MARCH 24

Sunny spring weather. It means more to Emily than to me.

∾

Reading another photography book—one fat with text. Trite bullshit mostly. Some very good pictures, though. Expensive ones of expensive people. Studios, lights, Hasselblads, assistants, make-up artists—not my sort of thing at all.

∾

Chicago train derailment leaves 32 injured.
Guinea scrambles to contain Ebola outbreak.

MARCH 25

Watching from the window as these packs wander home from school, it is not hard to spot the problem children, the ones who will eventually be identified (rightly) as bad influences—the pushers, the shouters, the nascent sociopaths.

∾

European stocks close higher.
Humans blamed for giant bird's extinction.

MARCH 26

Went with Emily to the hospital to fill out forms and have pre-surgery blood test and EKG. This is supposed to save time, but we know it won't. We will be answering these same questions and filling out these same forms again on the 9th when we check in.

Christine has come back to the subject of my reception. She cannot believe it does not bother me. Either I am not telling her the truth or there is something wrong with me. (Why does it have to be either/or—can't it be a little of both?) Do I want the music to be more broadly disseminated? Yes. Do I want it to be liked? Yes. Would I like more money? Yes. Would I like to be better known? No. Would I like to be invited to parties? No. Would I like to be on television? No. Would I like to do more interviews? No. Would I like to be treated differently by my agent? A little.

Girl scout sets record with huge cookie sales.
Winterhawks beat Vancouver for 3-0 series lead.

MARCH 27

Beth. Am again weighing pros and cons of continuing with her. She gives me the haircut I want (and have rarely gotten elsewhere), but she depresses me. Her place depresses me. Her dog depresses me.

Two firefighters killed in 9-alarm Boston fire.
California state senator arrested on corruption charges.

MARCH 28

Christine's father is one of those people you make allowances for—like someone with a metal plate in his head.

∾

Rescanned rough draft of short string piece and am discouraged.

∾

Astronomers spot one-of-a-kind asteroid.
Diet drinks linked to heart disease.

MARCH 29

Movie. A comedy I expected to walk out of, but ended up liking very much. Surreal nuttiness. A sort of updated Marx Brothers thing.

∾

Ham sandwiches for dinner.

∾

White House calls for new rules to cut methane emissions.
One million jars of peanut butter trashed.

MARCH 30

Took walk around Commonwealth Park.

∾

Have, I think, a genetic predisposition to dipsomania. Have flirted with it regularly.

∾

Powerful flare erupts on the sun.
Paris gets first female mayor.

MARCH 31

Have to get rid of the Buckley book. Some good photography in it, but it is overwhelmed by the prose—by a tsunami of self-indulgent, self-aggrandizing, touchy-feely bullshit. Give the man a camera, but please, someone take away his word processor.

∾

Note to self: Worry less.

∾

Four hurt, 200 evacuated in NW Pipeline plant blast.
Female circumcision on the rise in the US.

April

APRIL 1

My turn to visit the dentist. Lovely time as always. Fifteen minutes early. Unfortunately, so was someone else—a middle-aged man who thought he would entertain the receptionist with a ceaseless stream of clever chatter. He was talking when I arrived and still talking when I was called back to the masked hygienist. I don't think he took a breath the whole time. Seemed to find himself utterly fascinating.

∾

NATO suspends cooperation with Russia.
Firefighter rescues 6-foot python from blaze.

APRIL 2

I never think about outer space anymore. Thought about it quite a lot as a child, but at some point I came to the conclusion that it was better for me psychologically to stop thinking about it if I could.

∾

Have thrown away another would-be piece. Simply do not have the temperament to compose a credible lullaby.

∾

Death toll rises to 29 in Washington State landslide.
Scientists say they know why zebras have stripes.

APRIL 3

Sometimes there is nothing less welcome than another piece of information. Please don't tell me today that we are out of milk or that the Supreme Court has just made it easier for a billionaire to buy a congressman.

∾

Kelly Something works in our local coffee shop. She has wild hair, a long neck, and eyes like an ocelot. For some reason Emily and I have become objects of her attention. She sits down with us at our table from time to time. Her strangeness may be authentic, but it seems to me more likely a contrivance.

∾

Fort Hood gunman kills 3 people, wounds 16.
Dog escapes Texas backyard, somehow gets to Ohio.

APRIL 4

There are few interiors I know more viscerally or hate more deeply than those of our nearby hospital. Its spruce-green hallways are filled with existential boredom, its mahogany-trimmed waiting rooms with despair.

∾

Meningitis outbreak claims three in Los Angeles.
Shrunken heads found in 91-year-old's home.

APRIL 5

Dinner with Jim and Mia. Last social outing for a while. They have a niece, who is interested in Elvis.

∾

Note to self: See about having porch painted.

∾

Skydiver dies trying to set world record.
US to evaluate role in Middle East peace process.

APRIL 6

Are there still people in the world today who study their horoscopes?

∾

Why have I written mostly in minor keys: the zeitgeist. Work in major keys was for another time—a time when confidence did not seem psychologically suspect.

∾

Afghan turnout at polls is high.
Priests and nun taken hostage in Cameroon.

APRIL 7

Christine wants to know if I read the article in Metro Magazine by William McPherson? I did. I think he is a very fine writer, but I have never read a piece of his that I did not think was too long. He puts a considerable amount of time and energy into gathering his information and assumes you will happily put in similar amounts of time and energy reading the gratuitously detailed result.

∾

Gas prices rise 5 cents in past 2 weeks.
Crews battle blaze near Longview nursing facility.

APRIL 8

I am not one of those handy people who tries to fix things, but one who, in the face of misfortune, succumbs almost instantly to despair. My reaction to things breaking, to things going wrong, is not proportional but pathological. I am regularly overwhelmed.

∾

Organic eggs in short supply at local groceries.
Actor Mickey Rooney dies at 93.

APRIL 9

Checked into the hospital at 5:30 A.M. for Emily's surgery. Head aching, stomach knotted, eyes burning. Prep nurse is energetic waif with a kindergarten-teacher's voice and demeanor.

∾

Surgery two hours. Wandered halls. Moss-green carpet. Doctor appears from sterile bowels of place and tells me everything has gone well. Shows me x-rays of the titanium spacers placed in Emily's back. They look strong and orderly. Made a dozen phone calls to pass on the news.

∾

Toyota to recall 6.4 million vehicles.
Students stabbed at Pennsylvania high school,

APRIL 10

Emily home. Exhausted and in pain. Rearranged the furniture to make things easier, more convenient. Medication every three hours. Recovery is going to take some time.

∾

Washington State sewage plant invites weddings.
Burglars gun down farmer as family watches.

APRIL 11

Mild spring weather seems mocking. Pills, naps. A little walking. A little bandaging. A little television.

∾

Heavy spending by conservative groups tilts Senate races.
Feds probe deadly Calif. school bus crash.

APRIL 12

Trying to read early collection of essays by Olivia Summers. In the beginning her style was almost parodistically dense—paragraph after paragraph stuffed with specificity, with product, place, and proper names.

∾

Total lunar eclipse coming Monday.
Armed men seize police station in eastern Ukraine.

APRIL 13

Had my first extended talk with Kelly this afternoon. Actually, it would be more accurate to call it an extended listen. I dropped by for a cup of the good stuff on my way back from the pharmacy. She is a nonstop, gesticulating, free associator. She knocked over my coffee. Frenetically apologetic.

∾

Space Station glitch could delay cargo launch.
Pet adoptions half off this week at OHS.

APRIL 14

Took Emily to Commonwealth Park for a change of scenery and a very short walk. Conjured another vat of soup.

∾

Russian fighter jet buzzes U.S. warship.
Florida woman attacked by bear.

APRIL 15

British period drama. Basket of fruit.

∾

Finished Offill novel. Found many things to like, but I was never taken into its world. Never had that special feeling. Found myself looking again at the author photo. It was taken at a flattering angle—from just above and to the right. Her hair is draped dramatically to the side in an unsuccessful effort to glamorize, to distract from the uninterestingness of the face.

∾

Boston relives infamous day of horror.
Cat saves woman in mobile home fire.

APRIL 16

More walks. More British drama.

∾

Received check for music review.

∾

Students trapped in sinking ferry.
Captured cannibals refuse to eat jail food.

APRIL 17

Christine thought it might be interesting to get my reaction to her writing so she left me a couple of essays to read. She thought my comments might be useful. Am very reluctant.

∾

Pair of silver gelatin prints arrived. Lovely as always.

∾

Emergency alert malfunctions during manhunt.
Gabriel Garcia Marquez, Nobel Laureate, dies at 87.

APRIL 18

Little outing to Jamison Park. Saw a blue heron, a Rastafarian, and a middle-aged lesbian with a motorcycle.

∾

Fire truck plows into California cafe; 15 hurt.
Underwater robot measures Antarctic sea ice.

APRIL 19

Short trip to the store and a quiet day at home.

∾

Note to Self: Have patio power-washed.

∾

12 million patients misdiagnosed each year.
Calif. delays decision on protecting gray wolf.

APRIL 20

Do we all have certain smells that register specially with us—things outside the normal range of attractive scents that for some peculiar reason are uniquely engaging? Perhaps. For me two scents come to mind—one loved (the smell of wet dog), one hated (the smell of new-mown lawn).

∾

Flavored cigars appeal to youth.
German Shepherd called to jury duty in New Jersey.

APRIL 21

Short outing to South Waterfront. A wasteland of great glass condos, as we remembered.

∾

The harp is the only instrument that is impossible in this day and age to write seriously for.

∾

Violence in Egypt kills 2 police officers.
Lyrid meteor shower puts on celestial show.

APRIL 22

Mrs. Hampton is afraid she is going to be sued by one of those people who make their living suing.

∾

Trip to discount store to pick up household supplies in bulk—paper plates, toilet-bowl cleaner, aluminum foil, etc., etc.

∾

Church deacon charged in 33-year-old murder.
Caesar's makes bid for casino in upstate N.Y.

APRIL 23

It bothers me that Pluto is no longer considered a planet. It isn't that I have lost something from my childhood (or not entirely anyway)—it is the comfort this admission of fallibility provides to those who would try to undermine our faith in science, our faith in fact.

∾

Search ends for missing Sherpas on Everest.
Woman wants $275K for Estacada duck attack.

APRIL 24

Brutality and banality—they are the twin clichés of contemporary photography. I have little interest in documenting either.

∾

South Sudan to free alleged rebel leaders.
Avalanche warning issued for Mount Hood.

APRIL 25

Chauffeured Emily to her hair salon. Waited in nearby diner. Cup of coffee, mediocre piece of marionberry pie.

∾

Lots of intrigue. Who will be taking over Thomas Foster's post as head of the Northwest Literary Alliance? Who will be the new face of local literature?

∾

Bombing kills 31 in Baghdad.
Chickens stolen from north Portland yard.

APRIL 26

No interest in games of chance. Eat faster than anyone I know. Prefer night to day and being inside to being outside.

∾

40% of the dog-walkers in this neighborhood are men. Only 5% of children-walkers are.

∾

Teen stabbed to death after prom date rejection.
Biker looks for false teeth on busy Spanish highway.

APRIL 27

Have to admit even at this late date that I am still not sure this project—this journal—is worth the time. Something happens when I pick up a pen. Thought thickens. Mental mudslide suffocates animating impulse. Nothing is left of synaptic show but smoke and dying embers.

∾

Car crashes through dance studio, 1 injured.
Rabbit heads left in two sisters' mailboxes.

APRIL 28

Took Emily to N.W. 23rd for an outing.

∾

As a boy I was a climber of trees. I still feel the urge from time to time. Vestiges, no doubt, of my evolutionary past.

∾

Working on a new piano prelude. Tentative title: *The Shriveled Hope*.

∾

Tornado watches in 4 states.
Fisherman reels in massive 805 pound shark.

APRIL 29

Haircut with Beth. May be my last. She is raising her prices. Good excuse.

∾

Yard work.

∾

New gelatin print arrived. Night shot of nearby woods with fog and light. Nice picture—if a bit romantic.

∾

When was the last time anyone asked me to sign a score for them? It was two years, three months, and eleven days ago—the last time I overcame my reluctance and appeared in public as a "composer."

∾

Okla. to execute 2 inmates tonight.
Camels confirmed as source of deadly virus.

APRIL 30

Sellwood. Antique shops.

∾

Started reading another acclaimed novel, and I am not yet captivated. I sense a cautiousness in the prose—a certain sort of acceptable and edgeless honesty. Author's paragraphs seem full of so many words. His movement across the face of his story is glacially slow.

∾

Note to self: Eschew gloominess.

∾

Family missing for 3 days found alive in swamp.
Homeowner mistakes guest for intruder, shoots him.

May

MAY 1

Annoying business over the rights to an old essay collection. Think it has been taken care of.

∾

Rebecca—one of Christine's friends—is (as always) impeccably decorated. Clothing. Jewelry. Each piece has been carefully selected and vetted. It is included in the look only after a rigorous reference check.

∾

Riot police and protestors clash in Turkey.
Ducklings trapped at Keller Fountain rescued.

MAY 2

Visited galleries. Only a few interesting pictures. Miles Goodwin.

∾

Note to Self: Look into biography of Rasputin.

∾

Nigeria says number of kidnapped schoolgirls still unknown.
British royals spotted at Memphis restaurant.

MAY 3

Wandered Hawthorne district.

∾

When was the last time I changed my mind about something important?

∾

Woke up to hectoring warble. D flat.

∾

Teen plotted to kill family, bomb schools.
9 arrested in Seattle anti-capitalist march.

MAY 4

It would be nice, I think, in this drab journal to have some symbolically significant *femme fatale* wander onto the scene for a paragraph or two—a representative of the life force, the happy ending—but I look out the window and it is *femme-fatale*-less. I see only dog-walkers and lawn-care people.

∾

California Chrome wins Kentucky Derby.
Man robs Ga. Waffle House with pitchfork.

MAY 5

Emily is back to work for the first time since surgery. She will do half-days for a while. Her stomach—which is always ruined by anesthesia—is still ruined so another week or so of imagining and concocting inoffensive soups.

∾

Violence escalates in eastern Ukraine.
Toilet hurled from soccer stadium kills fan.

MAY 6

Emily knows a man at work by the name of Andrew Fenton. She is always trying to fix him up. The women she tries to fix him up with are mostly divorced and peculiar. She doesn't think he will notice since he is divorced and peculiar himself.

∾

Received notice that the last quartet was named a finalist for a small indie music award. Missed the cash prize, but I will be getting a certificate and a medal.

∾

Super-heavy element 117 confirmed by German scientists.
Naked man doing push-ups in the street hit by car, killed.

MAY 7

Squeezed in downtown photo walk. Came away with a couple of decent pictures—shabby-genteel buddies wearing beat-down fedoras and a lone, by-gone-era movie idol (continental-looking guy, cigarette hanging contemptuously from his lips).

∾

Stunt pilot dies in Calif. air show crash.
Chemical in kids' shampoos linked to cancer.

MAY 8

Big breakfast, then off for checkup with the doctor who did Emily's surgery. Everything is looking good.

∾

A man named Jeremy Buckman has been anointed head of the Northwest Literary Alliance. He is one of those people who knows people—not just any people, but the right people. It is the foundation of his appeal. The more right people he knows, the more right people he gets to know, and the more right people he gets to know, the more valuable *he* is—to know.

∾

Landmark Syrian hotel destroyed by rebels.
Foot in sneaker found on Seattle waterfront.

MAY 9

Received personal invitation to a new show at the Fowler Gallery. Not sure how I was selected for this honor. The "artist" is not one I have ever had any interest in. She is one of those wearying appropriationists. The work itself is secondary—an illustration. It is the gimmick—the self-promoting, gobbledygookish explanation of the work—that is most important.

∾

Mail-order chicks infect 63 people.
Police baffled by man's beheading.

MAY 10

Short walk in Waterfront Park. Ran into a festival of dogs—a benefit supporting the Humane Society.

∾

Bought a small bench for Emily's office. Required a little putting together. Gave me a chance to get into my tool box and commune imaginatively with an orphaned sense of primal imperative.

∾

Advanced prosthetic arm approved for US market.
National Football League's draft full of surprises.

MAY 11

Walked around lake at Commonwealth Park. If it weren't for the screaming children on the playground a hundred yards away, it wouldn't feel like we were in the city at all.

∾

Moral outrage—it seems such an easy way to anoint one's self. Cannot, at the moment anyway, think of a suitable alternative however.

∾

Iran nuclear deal takes shape.
Bears suspected in New Hampshire car break-ins.

MAY 12

Started to read again about the Bloomsbury Group last night, but stopped almost immediately. I am simply surfeited. This clique has never been an obsession of mine and has become an annoyance in its ubiquity. I don't think there is really anything of significance left to be said about them. It's possible, I suppose, that a trove of trivialities may be unearthed some day, but at this stage in the heliography that seems unlikely.

∾

Mrs. Hampton has never been on an airplane. Just the thought of one is enough to make her hyperventilate.

∾

Explosion in Indian embroidery factory injures 33.
Paving project slows Bethany Blvd. commute.

MAY 13

Sent Peter Cole a copy of my fifth quartet because I thought he might enjoy it and maybe give it a mention in his magazine. Unfortunately, he did like it and wanted to do an interview. I had to decline. I make these overtures from time to time—when I find myself feeling like I should—but I have never made one yet that I did not almost immediately regret as I regretted this one. Sent Cole a note asking him to forgive me for wasting his time—I did not do so intentionally. Both my music and my photographs will have to speak for themselves.

∾

Intimations of summer—the lawnmowers, edgers, and leaf-blowers are in bloom. It is the sound of a suburban morning. Landscaping companies roam the neighborhoods, contractual obligations honored.

∾

Scientists discover "metal-eating" plant in the Philippines.
Francis Bacon work could bring $80M at auction.

MAY 14

Christine accompanied Emily and I to a party for Val Wilson, who has just published a new book. The party was held at a very nice restaurant—a sign, Christine said, of the publisher's commitment. Dinner and gone. Minimal amount of postprandial schmoozing.

∾

Once again this morning the whisper in my ear—the meaningful moment to be preserved.

∾

Two miners die in West Virginia collapse.
NASA spots worrisome Antarctic ice sheet melt.

MAY 15

I can't remember the last time I went swimming.

∾

Cancelled appointment with Beth. Have to start looking for a new haircutter. One without a depressing Chihuahua.

∾

Note to Self: Look up medical description of epilepsy.

∾

Ohio measles outbreak biggest since 1996.
Feds charge Qualcomm managers with insider trading.

MAY 16

Andrew met one of Emily's fix-ups at a coffee shop downtown—a young lady named Jane Tower. They had a nice chat. The subject was dogs. They both liked them, but did not at the moment have one. They did, however, intend some day to have one and had ideas about the naming of this notional companion. There were, for each, a large number of possibilities, but in the end it seems to have came down to "Sam" for him and "Lucy" for her.

∾

India's opposition leader sweeps into power.
2 injured when crane overturns in Boston's North End.

MAY 17

Reading a new collection of stories by one of my favorite contemporary writers, Rachael Glass. She is brilliant, gifted. She has not created an extraordinary book so far, but it is in her power and I hope that someday she will—that what needs to come together comes together and that the distractions of the day do not circumscribe her promise.

∾

Saw a documentary on photographer Vivian Maier. Was on the decent side of middling. Could have been trimmed a bit, but a revealing look at the mystery woman—the eccentric who kept her work and her life private and was discovered by accident just after her death.

∾

Russian rocket crashes after takeoff.
Kraft recalls 1.2 million cases of cottage cheese.

MAY 18

Spent several hours buying a new couch. The old one has been sagging and is a bit frayed along the bottom. We will like the new one better than the old one, I think, but it is not so drastically different as to seem exciting.

∾

California Chrome wins the Preakness.
Lawn care error kills most of Ohio college's grass.

MAY 19

Made arrangements for a trip to Chicago in October. Great city. It's been a long time since we've been there.

∾

Marysville neighborhoods flood during storm.
Calif. mom accused of assaulting daughter's bully.

MAY 20

Emily's first day at physical therapy. Lots of bends and stretches.

∾

We have known the Nadell's for twenty-five years and marvel always at the complexity of their financial lives. Our financial lives are simple—foolheartedly so, I suspect. Both our assets and investments are breathtakingly mundane. Neither of us has ever been the least bit interested in sophisticated fiscal maneuvers. We know nothing of fungibles, non-fungibles, credit-swaps, or derivatives.

∾

Thailand army declares martial law.
Woman walks for help after bear attack in Alaska.

MAY 21

Noticed on the way to the mailbox today the saturated color of the sky. A blue that has no name. The clouds—they seemed almost contrived. Perfectly formed, ideal white.

∾

Note to Self: Put chairs in attic.

∾

Dodger prospect bites off teammate's ear.
Target fires president of its Canadian operations.

MAY 22

Dinner with the Caldwells at our favorite restaurant in the Pearl. We haven't seen them in a long time. As always, it seems when catching up we discover someone we vaguely know has been diagnosed with cancer.

∾

Head of the Homeowners Association is selling his house. Expect a lot of nothing from the new head. Little commitment to the place and no obvious agenda.

∾

Pakistan launches airstrikes against militants.
Scientists unravel termite's genetic code.

MAY 23

Lunch today with Emily, who afterward suggested a walk to the drugstore. I agreed because I knew there was drugstore stuff we needed, but I was not excited at the prospect. I do not like the drugstore—the fluorescent lighting, the items on offer reminding you of the thousand natural shocks that flesh is heir to (fevers, coughs, rashes, athlete's feet, hemorrhoids, ear-wax buildup). In truth, as I think about it, when it comes to stores—other than junk shops and galleries—I am never inclined to stay in one any longer than is absolutely necessary.

∾

North and South Korean ships exchange gunfire.
More storms, tornadoes possible in Colorado.

MAY 24

Wandered through City Fair in Waterfront Park. The games and rides are one thing, but the food—its appeal is unimaginable. Deep-fried lasagna, for instance.

∾

Still reading RG. Some of the work has devolved into a symbolic surrealism that is, quite frankly, boring. Following a hypothetical forever, a "what if" of something that could never be, for lessons about "what is" is tiresome. Fantastically constructed metaphors are never as powerful, engaging, or instructive as the pedestrianly real that occur in nature.

∾

Vegas man guilty of dancer's grisly murder.
Dust storm pileup claims 6 in New Mexico.

MAY 25

Documentary on Ralph Steadman, cartoonist/artist. Left after about a half-hour. Tedious. An all bells-and-whistles sort of film.

∾

Feeling low. How long before they concoct a chemical that makes such a mood obsolete—that renders it an historical curiosity, the psychological equivalent of scurvy?

President makes surprise visit to Afghanistan.
California gunman targeted sorority.

MAY 26

Decided on a new title for the quartet—one that at the moment seems perfect. Am relieved. I did not like the old title. Reluctantly accommodated it as I awaited superseding inspiration.

∾

Note to self: Consider an essay on the complexities of title selection.

∾

Train accident kills 40 in northern India.
Naked man playing violin at courthouse arrested.

MAY 27

Andrew told Emily today that it was not going to work out with Jane. As usual, he would not say exactly why. This means Emily will be back on the lookout for him.

∾

Saw new show at the Travers Gallery. Yet another exhibition of glorifying sanctimony—the concerned photographer's daring and noble opposition to depredation, oppression, and tragedy.

∾

Police locate veteran suspected in Florida triple murder.
World equity indexes up on US data.

MAY 28

Emily had lunch with an old friend from law school who decided many years ago when she graduated to have adventures. She is at present stationed in Sri Lanka (which she described as “moldy”) where she lives with a Russian ballet dancer she met in Moldova. (He looks after her dog.) Emily loves these stories as she herself has a strong inclination to itinerancy. (As opposed to me, who never wants to go anywhere and has a strong inclination to situate.) Her enthusiasm was damped a bit by the stories of bugs and rot, but her spirit is indomitable.

∾

Army of hedge-trimmers destroyed afternoon work session.

∾

Fire at hospital for elderly kills 21 in S. Korea.
US to reduce troop strength in Afghanistan.

MAY 29

Andrea Paulson (friend of a friend of a friend) lives in a very contemporary world—one of fashion magazines, cosmetic surgeries, divorce settlements, and sexually-transmitted diseases. Her consciousness is catastrophically constricted.

∾

Deadly pig virus hits farm for second time.
Captain missing after huge oil tanker explosion.

MAY 30

Emily had second physical-therapy session. Backs are a tricky thing. Exercise still very light.

∾

Starting another short piece that I cannot imagine will "delight" the right combination of tastes to become even momentarily visible. It is, I think, because of the strange things I do, mostly just a matter of luck.

∾

Kremlin advisor steps up war of words with US.
Store owner, 89, swats robber with a golf club.

MAY 31

Took car into dealership for regularly-scheduled service. I am treated extraordinarily well. It is apparently part of owning this nice car—a nicer car than we have ever owned before or will ever own again. I am referred to not as a customer, but as a guest (a tactic that does not accomplish what it is supposed to as I am antagonized, not assuaged, by the cynical deployment of euphemism). When I pick up the car it has been washed and the gas tank filled. I am given a small silver box of chocolate truffles as I leave.

∾

Note to Self: Consider seeing a professional.

∾

National spelling bee championship ends in a tie.
41 charged in insurance scam involving dead deer.

June

JUNE 1

Spent most of the day hunting for plants to replace the ones we lost in the protracted winter freeze.

∾

Newspaper owner among dead in jet crash.
115 lb. woman wins Illinois hot dog eating contest.

JUNE 2

Christine is talking again about my uneasiness with her. There are questions between us, I think, of sympathy and sincerity.

∾

Filling a few staves with sonata-like scratchings. Nervous stuff. Staccatissimo.

∾

Spain's King Juan Carlos to abdicate.
Police confiscate $3M worth of shoes from Ky. home.

JUNE 3

Looks like the new haircutter, Melanie, is going to be just fine. Thirty-something, suspiciously tan, small diamond stud in her nose. Has dogs, a fiancé, and a pleasant way. Wish I had abandoned Beth a year ago.

∾

President pledges solidarity with Eastern Europe.
Florida judge accused of punching attorney.

JUNE 4

Set up dinner with the Greens for the end of June.

∾

Another sad photography show. The fine art establishment (a cabal of vested interests) is not doing the medium any favors as it has relegated "visual interest" to the philistinic scrap heap. In photography, as in painting, I want to see something I want to look at. I do not want some ancillary item, some illustration of some narcissist's half-baked idea of intellectual profundity.

∾

Pakistani political leader is arrested in London.
Police round up runaway sheep in Sherwood.

JUNE 5

Walk along the waterfront. Navy ships in for the Rose Festival. Good crowd.

∾

Nicole Scott has had her hair cut short. Her stylist tried to talk her out of it, said she did not have the right shaped face for the cut she wanted, but Nicole insisted. It was not about optimizing her attractiveness, she said, it was about trying something new.

∾

Read another RG story. Confirmed what has come to be my basic opinion: 1. she is the most gifted writer working today, 2. she should not be writing fiction.

∾

Note to Self: Oil hinge on shower door.

∾

GM dismisses 15 in wake of troubling recall report.
Bill would make salt water taffy NJ's state candy.

JUNE 6

Pair of portfolio prints arrived from the Massachusetts lab.

∾

Received a new contract to do freelance work for the newspaper. I will sign it, but doubt I will be doing anything for them any time soon.

∾

Packed up for a short trip to the coast. Staying in Astoria.

∾

Reading an idiosyncratic history of photography. Impressed by the scope and the graciousness of the critiques. Would, of course, have preferred something a little less ecumenical. Lots of trivial posturing gilded or given a pass.

∾

D-Day veterans honored on 70th anniversary.
Alligator removed from Mississippi pool.

JUNE 7

Cannon Beach. First lungful of ocean air is therapeutic. Breakfast at Lazy Susan—oatmeal waffle topped with strawberries and bananas. Good, but ordinary-ish. Nothing like the winter offering—gingerbread topped with pears and lemon sauce. Yasmine has had her baby and is all thin again—though says she still has five pounds to lose. Can't remember the last time I met a woman (baby or no baby) who didn't think they had five pounds to lose.

∾

Astoria. Visited the River Gallery to see a retrospective show of an old friend, Harry Bennett, who died two years ago. Local character. Much loved. Full of life. Wonderful man. Borrowed his late style from Soutine.

∾

President opposed to Scottish independence.
Silverton man accused of killing neighbor's dog.

JUNE 8

Cannon Beach for the day. Unusual bicycles parked outside of Mike's. Heavy black frames. Fat, oddly treaded tires. Not like anything either Emily or I have ever seen before. Sort of thing you might expect a barbarian to ride. A man from the shop (maybe Mike) stepped out to tell us all about them. He went on for a long time about the unique nature of gearing mechanisms. I pretend to know what the hell he is talking about because I am still on many occasions polite. Last time I was on a bicycle was in Bruges. That was four years ago. A whim. Enjoyed it but do not, at this moment, expect to ever be on one again.

∾

Hood strawberry season at its peak.
3 students arrested in string of bomb threats.

JUNE 9

Vintage Hardware, one of my favorite places in Astoria, is basically gone. It was housed in the crumbling remains of an old hotel that was itself as interesting as the inventory. They have moved into a shiny new building by the water and are now more or less just another store. They are still stuffed with peculiarities, but they are cleaned-up peculiarities that are organized and situated in well-lit rooms. When you enter, the step you take back in time is now a smaller one.

∾

South African president in hospital for tests.
Water main break closes Cedar Point amusement park.

JUNE 10

Saw a photo by Paul Berthier taken in 1865. Figure study: fleshy nude seated on a featureless chaise in a featureless room with her back to us. She has a small bruise roughly the size of a quarter on her right thigh. Found myself wondering immediately how she got it and found myself interested immediately in the fact that I was interested in knowing this—in knowing how this woman, a complete stranger, was bruised 150 years ago. It is the temporal issues of photography that invariably beguile me—the existential subtext. Part of my problem with nature photography is that it is supposed to be timeless. Mountains, trees, rivers. For me, photography is always about time. Time and light. They are the foundations of the medium.

∾

Brothers accused in serial burglaries.
World's oldest man dies in NYC at age 111.

JUNE 11

Nicole's husband does not like her new hairdo. It confuses him. He doesn't know this new woman—this short-haired person who sounds like his wife. What was next—yoga?

∾

Worked on a handful of the pictures I took at the coast. Unhappy about the fate of Vintage Hardware, but I might have found a new subject—a brewery that has recently opened in an old cannery building. The vats are spectacular—tall, stainless steel, all light and geometry. The shots remind me of Leger.

∾

Sun unleashes two X-class solar flares.
Utah man accused of chaining 6-year-old son to bed.

JUNE 12

Christine wants to talk about my age. Do I mind being as old as I am? How does it affect the way I work, the projects I take on, what interests me? Important questions, I think, but I'm not going to be exploring them with her.

∾

Concert, Emerson Auditorium. Bach cantata, Debussy's *First Rhapsody,* and newly commissioned piece, *Last Exit* by John Wiley (all strings, no keyboard).

∾

Priest shot dead in Catholic church attack.
Senate race in Mississippi exposes cultural rift.

JUNE 13

Landscaper over to survey minor yard renovation and repair. Going to be expensive, but it needs doing.

∾

Have been thinking lately of setting to music a poem by Yeats—*The Second Coming*. Its resonance for me has always been uncommonly strong as I am congenitally predisposed to embrace firmly all bleak and apocalyptic visions. Can already hear the double bass—the sonorous, low C growls of rough beast slouching toward Barstow.

∾

Greek authorities seize record 1.1 tons of heroin.
Baltimore police shoot cow running loose in city.

JUNE 14

Another day of dispiriting news from Washington, another day of deploring what money has done to this anemic democracy. The more I watch of what is going on, the more I fear for the future that we as a republic will not survive this age of greed and idiocy.

∾

Shiite militia seizes control of Iraqi town.
Drunk honeymooner punches flight attendant.

JUNE 15

Gay Pride Parade. More colorful than the Grand Floral Parade. Cloudy at the start, but then drizzle and finally rain. Took a few pictures as always. The proliferation of subcultures fascinates me.

∾

200 sheep dead in Oregon truck crash.
Arizona man arrested for shooting at the moon.

JUNE 16

Reading Barthes. When people like him throw up their hands and say of photography that it is "a magic," it behooves people like me (people who might use a word like behoove and innocent others) to pay attention. There is at the center of the medium a great mystery.

∾

Bionic pancreas shows promise for Type 1 diabetes.
Crews pull horse from Salem mud hole.

JUNE 17

Working again on the quartet. End of first draft in sight.

~

As a composer I understand my voice, its relationship to me. As a photographer it is a trickier business. There is still a voice. It is individual, and it is mine—an identifying unity that is subtle and unarticulatable. Its relationship to me is more nuanced, more resistant to summation.

~

Eight members of militant group arrested in Spain.
Woman escapes after captor gets drunk.

JUNE 18

Took a picture today of pigeons. They were lined up on a railing along a wall near the square. Something about them caught my eye. I passed by easily the first time, but walking back a short while later I stopped and acquiesced to the impulse. A middling photo.

~

Syria bombing kills 20 in refugee camp.
World's rarest stamp sold for huge sum.

JUNE 19

Lunch with writer friend Michael Robin. We spent time as we always do complaining about the state of contemporary literature in general and the state of the short story in particular. Neither one of us like very much the workshopped tastefulness that has dominated the genre, but we are both a little worried about what is being praised as a revitalization—the magical realism-ish cartwheels now being done by a few high-profile practitioners. This reliance on fabulism—it is equivalent to cinema's craven reliance on special effects.

Oregon Historical Society honors wine industry.
Fourth-grader to sue classmate for bullying.

JUNE 20

The energy I put into the quartet and into taking pictures—is it too much or too little? There is dedication and there is delusion. Is there something in between—something perhaps made up in equal parts of both?

Yard work. A brush with nature. I am city streets, not a country path person.

Attacks by Islamists kill 47 in Kenya.
Diet to blame for mysterious birth defects.

JUNE 21

Movie. Australian post-apocalyptic thriller. Too much silence. Too much soulful staring.

∾

Tom, a narrow-minded and reflexively belligerent neighbor, has sold his house and moved to Montana (where, I assume, he will live with a tribe of narrow-minded belligerents very much like himself). Met him only occasionally, but it's nice to have him out of our lives, to know we will never have to see, hear, or think of him again.

∾

Note to self: Have lining replaced in leather coat.

∾

Pope Francis excommunicates Italian Mafia.
Mutt named Peanut wins World's Ugliest Dog contest.

JUNE 22

Mrs. Hampton will not swim in the ocean. There are sharks, jellyfish, and barracuda.

∾

Lunch with Carol Gish. Is there anything less inherently interesting than someone else's dreams?

∾

Hong Kong holds referendum on democratic reforms.
Pesticides suspected in metro area bee deaths.

JUNE 23

Nicole has purchased a new ensemble. It is not like anything she has ever worn before. She is debuting it at lunch with her good friend, Kim McCormick. Kim likes everything Nicole does—everything she buys, all of her states of mind, all of her various identities.

∾

US student trapped in vagina sculpture.
News Corp selling community newspaper business.

JUNE 24

Cleaning people in. A first for us. We have never had cleaning people before. Feels decadent. Scent of bleach in the air.

∾

New details surface on missing jet pilot.
Florida man falls into wood chipper, dies.

JUNE 25

Kelly Newhall has lost her wedding ring. There is much to-do. No one but Emily knows at the moment. It is a symbolic and financial catastrophe (the thing was a carat and a half), one that is likely to start a bigger conversation.

∾

Offered generous compensation (and guest room [with private bath] at esteemed professor's home) for performance and discussion of *Angry Sonata*. Declined for the usual reasons.

∾

5 shot at Mass. birthday party.
Stocks edge higher.

JUNE 26

Started putting together a new photo book. Can see in the preliminary mock-up the outline of my predisposition.

∾

Teen killed grandmother at nudist camp.
Bronx mystery creature is member of weasel family.

JUNE 27

Started reading a collection of essays that I have resisted for quite a while. Three problems approaching the book: 1. Cover decorated with big-shot endorsements (suggesting encomia related more to connection than to content), 2. author photo (grinning huckster with cheesy mustache),

3. author's first name (from another century, conjures up images of a none-too-bright Midwestern uncle).

∾

Floods force evacuation of 200,000 in Paraguay.
Miss Delaware, 24, loses crown for being too old.

JUNE 28

Dinner with Jim and Mia at a new place in the neighborhood. Food good, prices high. Don't expect it will last long.

∾

Sarajevo marks 100 years since Archduke Ferdinand shooting.
Missing dog, "Chichi," found on Barnes Rd.

JUNE 29

Some ideas, like certain bronze sculptures, develop an alluring patina over time and become more beautiful, more interesting with age. Wish this was the case with the quartet I am working on. At times the process seems reversed.

∾

Rescue worker dies trying to save fallen hiker.
Costa Rica defeats Greece on penalty kicks.

JUNE 30

Emily back at physical therapy for a new set of exercises. Diligent. Optimistic. Receptive.

∾

Another night of syncopated doubts.

∾

I was deformed, I think, by three experiences: an encounter with the concept of infinity, photographs of the Holocaust, and divorce.

∾

Note to Self: Be patient.

∾

Vendor accidentally shoots woman at gun show.
New species of mouse with elephant genes discovered.

July Again

JULY 1

The Needhams, Barbara and Jeremy, have very different tastes in movies and music. She—who is infinitely more open and adventurous than he—has tried to accommodate her husband's enthusiasms, but has not been able to. She cannot abide the movies he loves (simple, characterless things full of explosions and special effects) or listen to his music in the car (twangy, right-wing, Southern country). She is thinking about seeing a professional, but is wary. She is afraid she might discover something she does not want to discover—that in finding a way to tolerate his tastes, she may lose her inclination to tolerate him.

France's ex-president held by police.
Utah man in jail after fight over pew space.

JULY 2

Emily's birthday. Flowers. Presents. Ice cream.

∾

Tropical storm Arthur to become hurricane by Thursday.
Bear rescued after head gets stuck in cookie jar.

JULY 3

Started reading another memoir. Turned out to be, of course, another catalog of complaints about mom and dad—another stockpile of exculpatory evidence. (Should be a subtitle for virtually all contemporary memoirs: *Exculpatory Evidence*.) It is not understanding that is sought, it is exoneration. The author thinks she is charming me, but with every paragraph or two I like her a little less. It takes some effort, in fact, to not actually hate her. She knows how to disguise an assassination.

∾

Helicopter crashes near Hagg Lake.
11 Honduran miners trapped in small gold mine.

JULY 4

Downtown. Loitered around the blues festival for a couple of hours.

∾

Pyrotechnics in the park.

~

Reading another story of RG's last night and was overwhelmed not by a passage, but by a portion of a passage—by its density, intelligence, semantic suppleness. Not sure I know any other writer writing now who could do this.

~

Germany summons US envoy over spy case.
116 year old Arkansas woman named oldest American.

JULY 5

Short trip down to Keizer to see Civil War re-enactors doing what they do—that is, re-enacting the Civil War. Surprised by how few Confederates were wandering about and by how many women.

~

4 killed in attack near Somali Parliament.
Michigan farm hosts 41st pit-spitting contest.

JULY 6

Worked on pictures from yesterday. One pretty good, I think—a scraggly, forlorn horse tied to a scraggly forlorn tree. Makes me think of Quixote's horse, Rocinante.

~

Ominous warning of oncoming heat wave, which for me is an ominous warning of oncoming depression.

∾

Woke up to ragged cackle. F flat.

∾

Western officials press for audit of Afghan election.
California man blows off hands with fireworks.

JULY 7

Ran into Spaulding's daughter. Not my favorite person. She is one of those "diagnosed" children—one of those who has been medicated and counseled, one of those who has been praised and passed on. She rarely seems to have a thought that does not include herself. It won't be long now, I think, before she develops an eating disorder. Cannot guess which way it will go—eating too much or eating too little, flirting with obesity or emaciation.

∾

2 men die in Idaho river trying to save boy, 8.
Finnish couple win quirky "wife carrying" race.

JULY 8

Doctor visit with Emily. Check up on surgery.

∾

At what age does one start buying toothpicks?

∾

Note to self: Learn lyrics to Gilbert & Sullivan song.

∾

Police kill cow that charged Wash. officer.
Man dies at South Dakota hot dog eating contest.

JULY 9

Free association—it tells us something, I think, but not as much as Romantics would suggest. The source is more likely to be pedestrian than paranormal—related more to the midday meal than to metaphysics.

∾

I am not a resilient person. I do not bounce back as quickly as most.

∾

Israel attacks 160 sites as death toll climbs.
Cat in central Florida goes wild; owner calls 911.

JULY 10

We share so much, Emily and I, but our approaches to life in general seem so very different. She seeks to change things; I seek simply to endure them. She has a faith in the efficacy of action that I do not. A great part of her energy is directed at transformation while the majority of mine goes to sustaining an unexciting equilibrium.

∾

Coast Guard rescues 3 on Oregon coast.
US stocks fall on Portugal worries.

JULY 11

Landscaper out to look at faulty sprinkler system.

∾

Another talk with Christine. She is trying out summary statements about me—wants to see how I react. Says she views my art as interstitial—falling between one acknowledged form and another both in music and photography. Sounds a little fanciful, but I do not object or consider her to be completely wrongheaded

∾

Water level at Lake Mead drops to new low.
Naked Seattle intruder recites scripture in home.

JULY 12

The 90+ degrees are here.

∾

Wander through Bastille Day celebrations in Director's Park.

∾

When was the last time I had a clear and intelligent thought? It was, I think, my junior year in college, BA—Before Ambiguity.

∾

Second lightning strike fatality in 2 days at Colorado park.
New Mexico judge elected by coin toss after tie.

JULY 13

Scheduled a picnic at Richard and Karen's place followed by boating on Lake Oswego, but an unexpected set of thunderstorms swept in (complete with lightning) so had to cancel. Will try again in early September.

∾

The life of a lie—is it longer these days or shorter?

∾

Bear wandering at Lake Tahoe beach, killed.
Rocket blasts off for International Space Station.

JULY 14

Spent the afternoon studying long-term financial prospects. Nothing to get excited about. Could be worse.

∾

Invited (in error, I assume) to be part of a symposium on trends in orchestration.

∾

Germany takes World Cup crown.
Gonorrhea outbreak in Spokane.

JULY 15

Haircut. Made adjustments. More off front and sides.

∾

Picked up a new set of test prints from a local lab. Look good. Less expensive than the Massachusetts lab, but I don't have much confidence in the place.

∾

Gunmen slaughter 25 in Iraq brothels.
Mystery illness closes Blue Lake beach.

JULY 16

Steve, the window washer, is here today.

∾

Who has time anymore for improvisation?

∾

Note to Self: Measure height of kitchen cabinets.

∾

Seattle man tries to kill spider, ignites house.
California approves fine for water-wasters.

JULY 17

Went through Berelowitz show at the Murphy Gallery. Yet another example of a sad trend—if you make a boring photograph big enough, you are making a statement, you are making art. The sort of thing you would pass over as a mistake at 4x6 is, at 40x60, an investment.

∾

3 die in dramatic bank robbery, gun battle.
Microsoft announces huge layoff.

JULY 18

Read story of a man with an anxiety disorder who, desperate for relief, had brain surgery. Six months later he developed an obsession with the country music of Johnny Cash.

∾

Japanese nuclear plant deemed safe, nears restart.
Hero dog saves sleeping deaf boy from fire.

JULY 19

Downtown. Lousy movie. Lousy sand-castle-building contest.

∾

How many cups of coffee have I drunk from this particular mug?

∾

Kidnapped 5-year-old killed in police shootout.
Firefighter loses hand to flesh-eating bacteria.

JULY 20

Yard work. Last of it for a while, I hope.

∾

Looking at quartet laying here and despair. Think I had a good piece in me, but just never came close to finding a way to get it out. Probably a common delusion, one that makes living with mediocrity easier. Who doesn't think they could have done better than they have? Only someone who has tried as hard as they could. Who are they? They are monsters.

∾

Explosion reported in Lakeridge restaurant.
Tattoo removal program offers fresh start.

JULY 21

Emily in early for office breakfast.

∾

Note to self: Worry less.

∾

Buzzard Complex fire kills cattle, threatens ranches.
Deadly mosquito virus reported in eastern Mass.

CPSIA information can be obtained
at www.ICGtesting.com
Printed in the USA
LVHW011243150520
655574LV00006B/572

9 781734 67596